JIM-DANDY

Also by Hadley Irwin

ABBY, MY LOVE
BRING TO A BOIL AND SEPARATE
CAN'T HEAR YOU LISTENING
I BE SOMEBODY
KIM / KIMI
MOON AND ME
THE ORIGINAL FREDDIE ACKERMAN
SO LONG AT THE FAIR
WHAT ABOUT GRANDMA?
(Margaret K. McElderry Books)

THE LILITH SUMMER
WE ARE MESQUAKIE, WE ARE ONE

WRITING YOUNG ADULT NOVELS
(with Jeannette Eyerly)

JIM-DANDY

Hadley Irwin

MARGARET K. McELDERRY BOOKS

Margaret K. McElderry Books
An imprint of Simon & Schuster Children's Publishing Division
1230 Avenue of the Americas
New York, New York 10020
Printed in the United States of America
10 9 8 7 6
The text of this book is set in Goudy Old Style.

Library of Congress Cataloging-in-Publication Data
Irwin, Hadley.
Jim Dandy / Hadley Irwin. — 1st ed.
p. cm.
Summary: Living after the Civil War on a Kansas homestead with his stern
stepfather, thirteen-year-old Caleb raises a beloved colt and becomes involved
in General Custer's raids on the Cheyenne.
ISBN 0-689-50594-9
[1. Frontier and pioneer life—Kansas—Fiction.   2. Kansas—Fiction.
3. Horses—Fiction.   4. Custer, George Armstrong, 1839–1876—Fiction.
5. Cheyenne Indians—Fiction.   6. Indians of North America—Fiction.]
I. Title.
PZ7.I712Ji   1994
[Fic]—dc20   93-22611

To Marvia, North Dakota librarian, who wanted to know what happened next

CONTENTS

Jim-Dandy   1

Cheyenne Jenny   9

Rabbit Stew   18

Going for Broke   39

The Sellout   56

Dandy's Boy   76

Moving Out   93

To Horse!   103

The Last Dance   116

Afterword   134

JIM-DANDY

Chapter One

As soon as I saw him, I knew he was mine forever even if I wasn't sure how long forever was.

The foal lay in the grass, the Kansas wind drying the mane still damp and matted against his neck. The mare licked him until he raised his head, sniffed, scrambled to his feet, and looked straight at me before he burrowed his head under the mare's flank and drew in her milk.

I doubted it would do any good, but I reminded Webb Cotter anyway. "He's mine, isn't he?"

"Dominion belongs to the Lord." His voice was dry as prairie grass.

"But it was my money that paid for the stud."

The half eagle, a five-dollar gold piece, had been the only thing left me by my real father, but there wasn't any reason to remind Webb of something he'd rather forget. I said the words more to myself than to him just to hear how they sounded. When you live with somebody who can go a whole week without talking to anyone but God, you start talking to yourself.

"The trouble with you, Caleb, is that you think of now instead of tomorrow. The colt will grow to till the land. He'll be a jim-dandy if he makes it through the winter." Webb already saw him hitched to a plow.

I crawled up on the fence and sat balanced on the top rail. "He's got to have a name." When I didn't get an answer, I went on. "Today's Sunday. I could call him that."

Webb wiped his hands, bloodied from helping with the colt's birth, against his pant leg and fixed me with that stare of his that froze words right in my throat. "The Sabbath is not for dumb animals."

I didn't want to name him Sabbath. I wanted to name him Sunday, but it was no use explaining. Webb never understood anything.

The mare moved and the foal jerked his head and looked at me like he wanted to see if I was still there.

"How about naming him Absalom?" We'd just finished reading about him and David in the Bible the Sunday before.

"That's no name for a horse." Webb swatted the mare's rump and moved up to stroke her neck.

"I could call him Ulysses after General Grant."

Webb looked at me and frowned. "There'll be no mention of generals on this place."

For Webb Cotter, those were a lot of words. I jumped off the fence and put another rip in my ragged shirt. I didn't care. I could have gone buck naked for all it mattered to Webb. The mare turned her neck around so far she was nearly bent in half and licked the colt's damp coat again while he sucked away. Even though he braced himself on spindly legs, he couldn't keep from dancing.

"He has to have a name." I thought about the graves out back of our sod house. My half brother was buried there. Only two days old, but he'd had a name.

"One name's as good as another." Webb turned away from the mare.

"We could name him what *you* said."

Webb stopped and looked at me. "What did I say?"

"You said he was a dandy. We could call him that. Dandy."

Webb nodded like it hurt his neck that I hadn't said something else wrong. I never understood why Ma had married him, except for his being a Quaker same as her. Maybe there hadn't been much choice after my father got killed at Shiloh and Ma and I were left in Fort Leavenworth. Webb sure wasn't who I'd have picked for a stepfather, especially after he moved us out west to homestead. Truth be told, he didn't like me any more than I liked him, though he'd never own up to it. I guess you'd say we were kind of accidentally stuck together like tumbleweeds in a fence.

"Call him what you will, but I don't want you down here stirring him up."

"I have to water them, don't I?" I tried to make my voice soft as Ma's when she reminded me of something I should have known.

It worked because Webb mumbled, "See that's all you do," before he walked toward the barn.

I watched him go and wondered why he looked skinnier from the back than he did from the front. When he walked toward me, he seemed big and strong. When he walked away, I could see the limp.

Ma told me not ever to ask about it, but one time I couldn't help it. Webb had me out chopping thistles on the worst July day I'd ever known. I was so hot and tired and mad I just up and said, "How come you walk that way?"

I thought he was going to whack me with his hoe, but after a second he leaned on it and looked off across the field instead.

"I mean," I tried to explain, "were you hurt in the war?"

I should have shut up right then and there, but sometimes when you find a sore spot, you can't help but keep on digging.

"I was a Quaker in Bleeding Kansas, against slavery, against war." His voice was prickly as the thistles we were grubbing out.

"Somebody shoot you?"

He barely nodded.

"You shoot him back?"

"Quakers do not fight." He picked up his hoe and whacked off five thistles in one big swoop.

4

Wasn't long after that he made me start reading the Bible out loud every Sunday. Funny, though, there was a whole lot of fighting in those stories.

Now I hung on to the fence, arms locked, my chin barely touching the top rail, and talked to the foal. "Your name is Dandy, you hear? You're mine no matter what anybody says." He looked at me, his eyes brown as chestnuts, like he understood.

I crawled between the rails and edged toward Dandy. I wanted to touch him so he'd know for sure he was mine. He was still sucking when I drew my hand down the length of his neck. His coat was soft as feathers on a baby bird. Slowly I ran my hand down his foreleg, then up again and across his back. He didn't move away.

Maybe he understood that we belonged together. Of course he couldn't tell me that. It was enough to know that he was *there* for me.

I wanted to put my arms around all of him and hug. I couldn't reach that far, so I settled for laying my head against his neck. The mare jerked and then I heard the stamp of boots and knew I was in trouble. For all Webb's belief in not fighting, he might change his mind when it came to thrashing me.

He stood by the fence, the mare's halter dangling from his fist. "Didn't I tell you to stay away from them?"

"I was just touching to see what he felt like," I said, trying to figure out which way to run—down through the lot or under the fence and up behind the soddy.

"Now get out of here and don't let me see you until it's time for Bible reading." He wasn't yelling, but his words were.

I hightailed it to the wagon track that passed our homestead and led through the open prairie to the fort thirty miles north. Out of sight of the house, I angled toward the river through the green buffalo grass. Usually, Webb would have found some work for me to do, but it was his Sabbath and even if there was no Quaker meeting to attend, Webb stayed out of the fields and so did I.

In summer the river wasn't much bigger than the creek that ran past our place, but it was lined with a ragged fringe of trees, about the only ones within a day's ride. It was one of Ma's favorite places. When I was too little to be of any use to Webb, Ma and I used to go there a lot.

We always sat under one special tree. It was bigger than the rest and its roots hung down over the bank like fingers grabbing into the earth. Even if Ma never complained, I knew she got awful tired of the wind that blew night and day across the plains. Down by the river she'd put her arm around me and say, "Wind was meant for trees. Listen, Caleb, and remember, when the leaves rustle, it's God whispering."

I didn't care too much about that. I liked the tree for a different reason. Its branches were just right for climbing once I was tall enough to reach the bottom one, and then I could make it all the way to the top and look for miles. It was a good place for pretending, something Webb Cotter wouldn't have approved of if he'd known.

I settled on the highest strong branch, my back against the trunk where the bark was worn thin from all my leaning. There was nothing to see but a herd of buffalo and a lone hawk circling over sleepy prairie dogs. When there's nothing to see and nothing to do and nobody to do it with, you pretend. I always pretended the same thing.

I'd squint my eyes and wait until I saw the flash of sun on bayonets far away. As they came closer, the solid tramp of feet shook the ground, and when the band began to play, the sound was so loud it blotted out the wind. The regiment came nearer, uniforms bright blue with gleaming gold buttons.

The officer leading the troops wheeled his horse and charged toward me, his saber shining as he held it high. I wasn't afraid because I knew he was my father and that he'd pull the horse up, rearing, sheathe the blade, then call me to come down and sit in front of him on the saddle before racing back to his command.

The clang of a bell carried to me now on the wind. Webb was calling me back for Bible reading—the only kind of work we did on Sundays. We were up as far as Job in our reading, and what with his boils and all, it wasn't my favorite story. Some of the names were hard to sound out, but when I wasn't sure, I made them up. Webb couldn't tell the difference. He couldn't read.

That night after supper I finished off Job without Webb's complaining even once.

"He was a good man," Webb said, putting the Bible back

on the shelf. When Webb *did* talk he never sounded like he was aiming the words at me, more like he was saying things to himself—only a lot louder than he needed to.

"If I was Job I'd have *done* something," I said. "He just sat around wearing gunnysacks."

"Job had trust and patience."

They sounded like a team of horses to me.

The Kansas plains got terrible lonesome during the day, but at night the whole place came alive if you listened hard enough. I lay on my straw pallet, a soft breeze drifting through the window along with the sound of cicadas rasping and sawing. Then a couple of frogs started talking to each other down by the creek. I couldn't sleep so I got up and stuck my head out the window.

A coyote wailed, and when a wolf started howling I got worried about Dandy out there in the lot, and the more the wolf howled, the closer he sounded. I slid out through the window real quiet hoping the mare wouldn't nicker. There was plenty of light to see by, but it didn't matter. I could have walked every acre of the homestead with my eyes shut.

The mare didn't pay me any mind when I crawled through the fence. Dandy was curled up in the grass and didn't move as I knelt beside him and ran my hand down his neck.

"You *are* a jim-dandy," I whispered. "And some day when we're bigger, there'll be just us two." He didn't wake and I figured he was tired from his first day of living so I stayed right there beside him until the sky lightened.

Maybe being born was just as hard as dying.

CHEYENNE JENNY
Chapter Two

That summer the Kansas sun lightened Dandy's bay coat to the color of autumn oak leaves, and when he ran he looked as free and wild as the buffalo grass that stretched between us and Indian Territory. It was a good thing the colt still needed the mare and that the fences were strong or he'd have run so far that only the wind could have caught him.

Almost every night I sneaked out to the lot, at least until nights got too cold. After that I was so lonesome inside on my pallet that I almost cried. Maybe I did once when I got to thinking about Ma. I reckon it takes a long time to cry someone dead.

That's pretty much how most of my time went—me hauling water for the horses, trying to do everything Webb thought up for me to do, and watching Dandy grow bigger every day. He still hung around the mare and stayed clear of Webb's mean cow pony that shared the lot. He paid attention to me, though, especially when I managed to filch some sorghum molasses from the house. I'd dip my fingers in it and whistle and it didn't take long for Dandy to learn that a whistle meant something sweet and good was waiting for him.

When fall came, he was alone, the cow pony and the mare busy pulling the breaking plow, digging black ribbons out of the prairie. Dandy crisscrossed the lot calling to his mother, but she plodded on as if he no longer existed. Maybe he missed his ma as much as I missed mine.

He learned to let me smooth down his coat with a curry-comb and straighten out his mane. Sometimes he'd rub his head right against my shoulder and then, when I was about to reach around his neck, he'd whirl on his hind feet and go dancing across the lot to the far fence.

The first time I got a rope around his neck was about the last time I saw him stand still. He came trotting up to the fence when I whistled and stood with his head high waiting for a taste of molasses and nipping at the collar of my shirt in case I forgot.

I had the rope, old and frayed, wound up around my arm where I figured it would look like just another part of my shirt. I crawled through the fence and held out my fingers so he could lick them, and with the other hand I slid the noose over his nose and up past his ears so it was hanging loose around his neck.

We were doing just fine until I started moving away and the rope tightened. Dandy didn't waste time bucking. He just leaped sideways and headed full tilt toward the end of the lot. One thing he didn't count on was me hanging on to the rope. One thing I didn't count on—how fast and strong he could move.

All I could do was dig my toes into the dirt. I went bouncing and jouncing and finally fell flat and was dragged along until I let go my hold. Off he ran, tail streaming in the wind, until he got as far away from me as he could. It took a good hour or more for me to get close enough to slip the rope off his neck before Webb Cotter got back from his plowing.

I didn't give up, though, and neither did Dandy. Every afternoon while Webb was in the fields, I'd manage to get the loop around the colt's neck, and every afternoon, with a flick of his ears, he'd be off and running, only I had more sense than to try and stop him until one time I didn't even bother to crawl down from the fence. He must have figured we were playing some kind of game and I was tired of it.

When he got to the far corner and I hadn't moved, he came trotting back, tossing his head, the rope trailing on the ground, and sidled right up beside me even if there wasn't any molasses to be had. After that he even got so he'd let me lead him around the fence line as long as I didn't pull the noose too tight.

That's when I started really talking to him, not just calling his name or whistling to get him to come to me, but talking like I hadn't talked since before Ma died. He couldn't understand the words, but it didn't make any difference because he looked like he could. His ears flicked forward and he turned his head to look at me with eyes like dark brown mirrors.

Mostly I talked about Ma and what it had been like while she was still there, back at the soddy. I told about how gentle her hands were and how she always smelled sort of sweet and soft like spring winds when they first come up from the south. I explained how she taught me to read from the only books she owned.

Once I even showed him the picture Ma had been working on before she took sick. I had it hid under my straw mattress for fear Webb would find it and get rid of it like he did all her clothes. I didn't think any horse, not even Dandy, could see the colors, but I showed him anyway. She'd made them herself out of plants she picked and boiled up, and she'd painted them on a smooth shingle left over from the roof.

Ma had said she wasn't making it up, that she was doing it from memory of a picture she'd seen once called "Peaceable Kingdom." The only part she had time to finish showed a white-faced steer and a fierce-looking lion sort of cuddled up to each other with a little kid in a white sheet hanging on to their necks. He stared straight out of the painting not even noticing a mean wolf and a woolly lamb curled up at his feet.

After Dandy figured out that the picture was nothing he

could eat, he snorted and went back to munching what grass was left in the lot, but it didn't matter because for a little while it was like Ma was still alive for me.

Winter came fast that year and when snow filled the air so you could hardly breathe, Dandy let me get him into our makeshift barn along with the other horses.

One cold morning Webb and I were cleaning the stalls when he said, "You might as well move in here and live for all the good you do around the place."

We were prying up clumps of frozen manure with big five-tined pitchforks. Webb dug while I carried outside and stacked. If we had to we could use the manure for fuel if the snows got too deep to find anything better. Dandy was stamping in the near stall.

Since Webb was less disagreeable when he thought I was working hard, I asked him what I'd been wondering for the last month. "How soon can I ride Dandy?"

"In another year, after he's broke."

The chunks were heavier and the trips outside longer. "I thought maybe in the spring." I stopped to catch my breath. Even in the cold Kansas wind, sweat was snaking down my back.

"Nope." Webb rested both hands on the handle of his pitchfork. "You don't ride a horse that young."

I knew it wasn't any use, but I tried. "I ain't heavy."

"Makes no difference," he growled. "Don't want a lame horse."

"I meant bareback, not with a saddle."

Webb bent back to work. "Stay off that colt. Understand." It wasn't a question, it was an order.

It wouldn't have done any good to ask why. His answer was always the same—"Because I say so!" I always wondered how someone who couldn't even read could know as much as Webb claimed to.

I turned toward the door with the last forkful of frozen manure—and standing just inside was an Indian woman, a shawl covering her head and falling down over her antelope-skin gown. I dropped my pitchfork.

Webb looked up, and seeing the woman, walked over to her and started talking in a strange language. The woman smiled and looked at me.

"Caleb," he said to the woman and moved his hands in a funny way.

To me he said, "Cheyenne Jenny. She and Dutch Bill run a trading post down by Wolf Creek."

"How do you do, Caleb," she said in a low monotone, her eyes never leaving my face, like she was memorizing me. She looked at Dandy and her eyes widened and she puckered her mouth as if she was going to whistle. Webb said something more that I didn't understand and she answered. I realized they must be talking Cheyenne.

"What's she saying?" I asked as the woman walked over to Dandy and, murmuring, ran her hands across his back. He snorted, but as the woman went on touching him, he didn't shy.

"She asked," Webb turned to me, "if this is the Morgan mare's foal."

"How does she know about your mare? She hasn't been here before."

"Bought the mare from her before I married your ma."

"Fine horse," Cheyenne Jenny said, forming the words separately as if they meant two different things.

"Tell Jenny his name," Webb suggested.

"Name." I paused. "Horse—name—Dandy."

"No need to talk that way. She understands English just fine."

"Dandy," the woman repeated and smiled at me.

Webb and the woman talked together in that other language, sometimes making motions with their hands instead of saying words. Then, as quietly as she appeared, she left, pulling her shawl close about her as she faced a blast of wind that made the lean-to shudder.

"What's a woman doing out here alone in the middle of winter?" The least Webb could have done was ask her to come up to the soddy and get warm.

"She wasn't alone. Probably some Kiowas or Arapahos waiting for her—down by the creek, maybe."

"Why did she stop here?"

"She wanted to tell me to look for trouble in the spring. Chief Black Kettle's all for peace, but his young Cheyenne warriors want to fight."

"What about?" In the whole two years we'd been living on the homestead no Indians had ever bothered us.

"Railroad's going through. They're losing their buffalo herds. Just like the cavalry, they think fighting solves everything."

"When did you learn to talk Cheyenne?"

"Picked up the little I know from Jenny when I worked at her trading post. Learned sign language first. All the Plains tribes understand that even if they do speak different languages."

"Could you teach me some words?" I never thought Webb could know anything I'd like to learn, but this was different.

"Don't know too many, but I could teach you to sign."

That winter, stuck inside the sod house as the Kansas blizzards howled across the prairie, Webb and I did more talking than we ever had—in sign language.

"First, forget English. From now to chore time, think Cheyenne," Webb began that day sitting cross-legged before our fireplace. "You sit down, too. Now," he went on, "the two most important signs are *I* and *friend*." He motioned toward his chest with his right thumb and said "I," then hooking his index fingers and looking at me almost like he meant it, said "friend."

After we'd "I-friended" a lot of times, we moved on to *peace*, after I finally got it through my head to keep the back of my left hand down. The sign for horse was easy because all I had to do was put two fingers of one hand astride the index finger of my other hand and make like a horse running.

That first day I learned the signs for *good* and *go* and *stay* and *water*.

I broke the rule of not talking and asked, "Is there a sign for *mother*?"

"Tap your heart twice," Webb said, gazing into the fire, "with your right hand closed."

"What about *father?*"

"Don't know." He stood and made the signs for *go* and *horse* and *water*.

I went and watered the horses.

RABBIT STEW

Chapter Three

No "Indian trouble" came that spring or in the summer that followed, at least not as far as anyone bothering us. Once when Webb returned from a trip up to Fort Hays to get seed and supplies, he said there'd been a big meeting between a lot of the tribes and some general, and it looked like maybe there'd be room for Indians and settlers and railroads in Kansas after all.

By the next spring, Dandy was two years old, I was thirteen, and Webb Cotter had used the money from last year's crops to buy another forty acres of land. I couldn't see the point in it myself. It never made sense exactly who he was buying it *from*. So far as I knew, we were the only ones around between Fort Larned to the south and Fort Hays to the north, which was probably why whatever else the Cheyennes were doing, they sure never bothered us.

That spring, when the rains washed out the frost locked deep in the fall plowing, the creek filled and roared, making a swamp of the land around it. Then the sky, rinsed clean of clouds, blued, and the sun burned through the June days. Wheat sprouted, broke through dry, cracked soil, and withered right back to where it came from.

That's when I learned Webb wasn't the only crazy home-steader in western Kansas. There was at least one other, and he showed up one morning and leaned against the fence. His name was Mason. He and his family had settled just a few miles away.

"Good-looking horse you got there." The man watched Dandy gallop the length of the lot and skitter sideways until he danced up next to where I was standing.

"Yep." Webb gave the man a quick once-over glance. "Ain't the ugliest I ever seen . . . quite."

"He'll be a stubborn one to break," the man went on.

"I'll break him," Webb muttered, watching Dandy without turning his head, just moving his eyes.

My stomach knotted when he said "break," crunching off the word like the sound of bones snapping.

"He'll be tough as a pine knot." Mason pushed back the brim of his hat. "Don't know where you got the stud, but some critters are born skittish and nothing a fellow can do about it."

"Anything can be broke. It just takes a strong, gentle hand." Webb fingered the corner of his mustache and turned toward me. "Thought I told you to fetch some water."

I took my time about moving.

"Your boy?" Mason asked.

"My wife's." Webb didn't bother to look at me. "Died two years ago." He wiped his forehead with the back of his hand and stared at the sky. "If we don't get rain soon, can't hope for much wheat."

If the water I was supposed to fetch was for Webb instead of the horses, I would have let him thirst to death. As it was, I grabbed a pail and went on to the creek. Even in the drought, there was a gush of cold water from the underground spring that pumped out enough for both us and the horses. Anybody else would have fenced the lot so the stream flowed through it. Not Webb. Guess he liked to see me busy carrying buckets.

What did they mean? Stubborn! Tough! Skittish! They didn't understand Dandy. Couldn't they see he wasn't ugly? The rest of him'd catch up with his legs someday. He'd fill out so his neck wouldn't look so gangly. And he wasn't skittish! He just didn't like to have all four hooves on the ground at the same time. When I got back Webb and Mason were walking down toward the field where winter wheat showed a few straggly green shoots—Webb a full foot taller and a good foot skinnier than the new neighbor.

It was July when Webb turned out the hobbled horses into the fields to grub what green they could find. The dwarfed shoots must have tasted brittle and bitter to Dandy, whose coat looked as dry as the wheat. The only thing he had enough of was water that I fetched.

Then one morning Webb announced, "I'm lending Mason the mare for his keeping an eye on you. Signed up for work on the Santa Fe Trail so I'll be gone for a spell."

He'd been gone a couple of times when money was short before Ma died, but that was only for whatever job he could pick up down at Larned for a week or so. Even I knew a trip to Santa Fe would take him over a month, and I wondered why he'd waited so long. We'd been needing cash ever since he bought that extra land.

"You need anything, you scoot over to Mason, you hear?" He got on the cow pony, the mare's lead rope in one hand. He looked like he was making up his mind to say something else, but instead rode away leading the mare.

A day later Mason showed up and with him came the dog.

"You can have him. He's the throwaway of the litter," he told me. "Don't worry about feeding him. He can fend for himself. Thin as a splinter—that's his name—Splinter. Part collie, part coyote and the runningest critter I ever seen. He grew up chasing tumbleweeds."

Splinter wasn't the only thing Mason brought that day when he drove up in a buckboard pulled by our mare.

I'd been so busy watching the pup race around in circles, I didn't notice the scraggy, straw-headed kid tagging along behind until Mason said, "And this here's Athens."

Blue eyes stared straight at me from underneath eyebrows bleached the same color as the hair.

I stared back. I'd never met any boys since we began

homesteading, but this one looked to be about my age, thirteen. I couldn't think of anything to say back that didn't sound dumb, so I just nodded and stuck my hands in my pants pockets like I'd seen Webb do when he didn't want to talk.

Mason watched me as he went right on, his words coming out as easy as if he was used to people listening. Webb never looked at me except when he was giving orders.

"Told Athens about you and the colt." He nodded toward Dandy, who'd come sidling up to the fence. "It's pretty lonesome out here and I thought you could use some company. I've got to go down to Larned and pick up some supplies. Maybe you two can get acquainted while I'm gone. What do you say, Caleb?"

"When do you figure to be back?" I'd planned on trying to get Dandy to settle into a slow walk as we made our daily round of the lot, but now I had two new things to put up with—a dog named Splinter, who still hadn't stopped running, and a boy who was frowning at me and looking mad before we even got to know each other.

"Should be back by sunset," Mason said.

By the time Mason got back in the wagon and drove off, I'd sneaked another look at the boy, his hands lost in shirt sleeves that were too long and wearing a pair of britches that looked like castoffs from his pa.

"What are you staring at?"

My face got hot and when I tried to swallow, I didn't have any spit to swallow with. "You're a girl!" I finally managed to say.

She watched me like I was as dumb as Splinter. "Of course I'm a girl. What else could I be with a name like Athens?"

"I never heard a name like that before."

"It's for the town where I was born, Athens, Ohio. Then we moved on west to Indiana. My sister Terry Haute was born there."

"You're both named after towns?" I wondered if Webb Cotter knew what kind of person was supposed to be keeping an eye on me.

"Sure. That way we all remember where we lived and when. We moved to Illinois next and—"

"You mean there's more of you?"

"Yep. That's where Normal was born. Normal, Illinois. We just stayed long enough for that to happen before we left for Iowa."

"And then . . . ?"

"My sister Pella."

"A whole family of girls?" There was something about her that wouldn't let me get a whole sentence out of my mouth.

"What's wrong with that? Pa says the hands that rock the cradles rule the world. I've seen enough cradles, but I like the idea of ruling." She looked up at the sky. "Think of sitting up there and ruling everything from Ohio clear through Kansas."

Just then Splinter squatted down, front legs flat in front of him, hind legs bunched up, nose sticking in the air like a howling coyote, and Dandy trotted over, stretching his neck and sniffing like he'd found something that might taste good if he took a nibble. They stayed still until Splinter flipped around fast as a jackrabbit and raced down the fence line, Dandy right behind. They tore around the lot and then switched directions so the dog was chasing Dandy.

"So that's your colt?" the girl asked.

"Sure is," I bragged. "His name's Dandy and I was just fixing to teach him to let me ride him."

"He hops around like a grasshopper in a heat wave." She rolled up the too-long sleeves. "Well, let's get started. What do you want to do first?"

First was easy, especially since Dandy stood still for once, catching his breath. It didn't take long to fetch the rope I had hidden and loop it around his neck. I made a big thing of leading him up and down trying to make it look like I didn't think he'd take off running any second.

Maybe it was because of Athens that Dandy was showing off as much as me, but he danced beside me as if we'd been practicing for months instead of weeks. After about five trips past her, I brought him up to the fence. I hoped he wouldn't take one close look and bolt away with me trying to haul him back. A good thing that Splinter got bored with the whole business right about then. He found a spot in the shade of the barn, flopped down flat on his side and, from the looks of his paws, was chasing rabbits in his sleep.

"What next?" Athens asked like she already knew the answer to her own question. "Have you tried sacking him out yet?"

I didn't want to let on that I didn't understand what the

heck she was talking about, so I shrugged and said, "No, but now's as good a time as any."

She was already headed for the barn and called back over her shoulder, "I'll look for a gunnysack. Where do you keep them?"

We had a few left from the seed Webb bought last spring, so I yelled back. "Inside the door on the right." I wondered what she was going to do with one.

She was back so quick I decided even if she was a girl, she could run as fast as me.

"I don't see a snubbing post." She looked around the lot and shook her head. "Maybe you mean to gentle him instead of sacking?"

Dandy watched her, ears forward, ready for another game of tag.

"That's been my plan," I told her as if I'd been thinking of it for months.

"Then we'd best start out easy." She snaked through the fence and walked right up to Dandy's head, the sack dragging on the ground. He blew through his nose, moved his feet, and didn't shy from her like I expected.

"Guess we could use a fence post, but maybe you'd better hold him instead. It won't seem so strange to him that way. I'll just put this on his back and see what happens."

I could have told her what would happen, but there wasn't time. The second he felt that gunnysack across his withers, Dandy was gone like a whistle in the wind. Good thing for me I wasn't holding tight to the rope.

"What'd you go and do a fool thing like that for?" It was

25

my turn to be mad, and the rope burn across my hand didn't help my feelings.

She was trying to keep her mouth straight, I could tell, and that didn't make things better. In a minute she said, "You never did see a horse sacked, did you?" Before I could lie, she went right on. "See, you tie him up tight to a post, so tight he can't jerk loose or throw himself on the ground, and then you flap the bejeezus out of him with the sack until he either learns to stand still or drops dead."

It sounded like something Webb would come up with when he said "break." That made me even madder. "We were going to gentle him. You said so yourself."

She didn't apologize. She bent down and picked up the sack. "We better try again. You fetch him and we'll start over."

It took a lot of coaxing and molasses and rope burns till he finally gave in and let us lay the gunnysack on him for more than a blink of his eyes. By that time we were tired and hot, so after watering Dandy we walked back to the shade of the sod house. Athens chose a bare spot and sat, her legs spread, and with both hands she smoothed a patch of dirt in front of her and drew a circle in the dust with her finger. Then she tugged at a leather thong hanging around her neck and untied a jackknife, a bone-handled knife with ends tipped in silver and slots for four blades, except all the blades but one were broken off.

She snapped open the lone blade, a long, thin, pointed, ugly blade, and balancing the handle up against her chin, asked, "Ever play mumblety-peg?" Without waiting for an answer, she gave the knife a flip. It arced through the air and came down with a quiver, sticking upright in the dirt, exactly in the center of the circle.

I didn't know any games except the ones I made up myself and if I'd had a knife, I wouldn't have wasted it that way.

Then she laid the knife on her closed fist and at a quick turn of her wrist, the knife flew through the air again and landed almost in the same place as the first time.

"That was the right hand. Now the left."

She did it again, the knife, like magic, sticking in the same spot.

"How'd you learn to do that?" I was beginning to think there wasn't anything Athens couldn't do and what was worse there wasn't anything I could do that she didn't already know how to do.

"Pa taught me. I can do it better with the other knife I have at home."

"You got two knives!" I didn't even have one. If I'd had anything worth trading, I would have offered it then and there.

"Sure." She handed me the knife. "Here. Try it, then we'll play one game and see how it goes."

I took the knife. It was cold and hard against my palm and fit like it was meant to be mine. After about a dozen tries I finally got the blade to stay long enough for Athens to call it a "sticker," even if it was clear out on the edge of the circle.

"Now this is the way we play." Athens smoothed out the dirt and redrew the circle. Reaching into a pocket, she pulled out a wooden peg, sharpened at one end and, using the handle of the knife, pounded the peg in the middle of the circle. "See, we take turns trying to hit nearest the peg."

"But you'll win. You've had practice." No matter how hard I tried, I couldn't keep the knife inside the circle let alone make it stay stuck.

"That's all right. The loser gets the peg."

"What do I do with a peg?" I was not liking the game. I wasn't too sure I was liking her either.

"You'll see. Come on. You start first." She sat back, arms folded, and watched as I flipped the knife and saw it skitter off beyond the circle.

"You're not doing it right." She took the knife, placed it on top of her head and gave it a flip. It nudged right up to the peg. "See? That's the way you do it."

"I see," I grumbled, carefully aiming my right-hand-closed-fist throw. The knife stayed in the circle, but it was what Athens called a "leaner."

"Almost a 'sticker,' though," she added. "You're catching on real fast."

It might have been a game to Athens, but I was not having fun. No matter how she flipped the knife, it sailed right in next to the peg. She missed only once when she tried to do it with her eyes shut.

I finally got one to stick inside the circle.

"Game's over!" she announced. "I won, but you get the peg."

"I don't want the old peg. You can have it."

"You're not playing fair. The loser *has* to take the peg." She snapped the knife shut and strung it back on the leather thong. "The loser has to pull the peg out," she smiled a nasty smile, "with his teeth!"

I felt like punching her right then and there and wiping the silly grin off her face, until I remembered what Ma used to tell me when I got mad and clenched up inside. "He who is slow to wrath is of great understanding." I hadn't known who Wrath was, but I knew now. Its name was Athens. I waited, but no understanding came. I finally got down on my belly, stuck my face in the dirt, and pulled out the peg. I handed it to her, spit out a mouthful of dust, wiped my face on my sleeve, and started for the barn.

"My pa's coming!" she shouted after me.

I looked off at the horizon and sure enough, I spied a cloud of dust that meant Mason was back from Larned. I thought real fast. It didn't take any great understanding for me to know that I didn't want her telling him about trying to teach Dandy and then have him tell Webb Cotter. It was face up to him or her.

I faced her. "Breaking Dandy is a big surprise for Webb, so it's a secret between you and me. We won't even tell your pa. What do you think?" I smiled, but it wasn't a nice smile.

She looked at me as if she didn't believe a word I was

saying. All the same she nodded, spit on her palm, and held it out to me. "I won't tell if you won't tell."

I spit on my own hand and we shook on it.

As it turned out, being alone on the homestead wasn't much different from when Webb was around except I felt better. I was free of having Webb always asking where I'd been or ordering me to quit lolling around and get busy doing something. The best part of being alone was I could do things I wanted to do without having to sneak around to do them.

A few days later I was sitting on the porch, my feet propped against the railing Webb had made for Ma after she took sick, when I saw three of the Masons coming across the field, Athens herding two little ones like she was a sheepdog.

"Pa thought you might like to come with us."

I couldn't forget what it felt like when she made me get down and stick my face in the dirt just because I'd lost a game. "I'm busy," I said, squinting into the sun like I was deciding what time it was.

"Doing what?"

"Thinking."

"I thought you said you were busy." She sat on the bottom step. "This here's my sister Pella and the little one's Topeka."

Pella, a miniature Athens, held the hand of a pudgy ball of a girl with a face full of fist who sucked on a thumb and looked up at me with eyes like a cat's through a maze of copper hair.

"Topeka?" I repeated.

Topeka moved the thumb to one side of her mouth and jabbered.

"What'd she say?" I looked down at Athens.

"I don't know. Ask Pella. She's the only one who can understand what she says."

Pella didn't wait to be asked. "She said she was born in Topeka."

"That's in Kansas," Athens added.

"I know," I answered, frowning.

"Well, I bet I know something you *don't* know."

"What?" I didn't really care, but somehow she made me ask anyway.

"I bet you don't know who can take a hundred people up to Fort Hays in one wagon."

"A hundred people in one wagon? Nobody can."

"Can too."

"There's not a wagon big enough."

"You're wrong. Anybody can." She stood up eyes level with mine. "Anybody who makes enough trips!" She laughed.

I didn't laugh.

"Don't you get it?"

"Of course I do. It's not very funny, though." I liked her less and less.

"It's a riddle. Don't you know riddles? Like—what's taller sitting down than standing up?"

I didn't answer. She wasn't going to get me to ask "what" again.

31

I didn't get a chance. She laughed so hard she could hardly talk. "Out there by the fence—Splinter."

"You mean a dog?" I couldn't help laughing this time.

"Tell you what I can do." I tried to make it sound important. It worked because she asked, "What?"

"I can throw up any time I want to."

"Let's see you do it then." She waited, hands on her hips.

I stood up, looked around, and finally shrugged one shoulder and said, "I don't want to." I laughed at *her* this time.

She looked at me for a minute, and, not bothering with spit, stuck out her hand. We shook. I figured we were even.

"Where'd you say you were going?" I asked.

"Checking our trap lines."

"What're you trapping?"

"Rabbits."

"Are they coming with us?" Topeka wasn't much bigger than a rabbit herself.

"Pella has to take care of Topeka and explain what she says. Besides, if you don't watch her she'll eat anything that doesn't eat her first. And I have to take Pella with me because she's the only one who can stand to kill the rabbit when we catch one."

I looked again at Powerful Pella. She smiled like she'd received a medal for bravery.

"Well, let's go," I said. "Where'd you set your snares?"

"Over by the river."

We started out, Athens leading the way, Pella tugging Topeka along by the hand not stuck in her mouth, me bringing up the rear, with Splinter already racing far ahead of us.

"You see," Athens said as we slid down the riverbank, "if we catch enough rabbits for stew, we get to have Christmas tomorrow."

"Tomorrow? But this is July!"

Athens didn't hear me. She was crawling up to the base of a big cottonwood tree. "Get your stick ready, Pella," she shouted.

Nobody said anything. Topeka stopped sucking her thumb. All I could hear was the rustle of the wind stirring the leaves. Athens pulled gently on the twine of the snare. "Empty!" she muttered. "Thunderation! We got to catch a rabbit or we can't have Christmas."

"Why are you having Christmas now?"

She sat up, her back against the tree. "Because we missed it last winter. Pa just sold some wolfskins and got enough money to get us all presents so we're going to celebrate tomorrow. We *always* have rabbit stew for Christmas dinner."

It made some sort of sense, I guessed, and when the next snare held a big jackrabbit, the noose tight around his neck, I was just as tickled as everybody else, except the rabbit, of course. I shut my eyes, though, when Pella finished him off and was glad Athens didn't notice.

"Hocomheeshuies," mumbled Topeka around her fist.

"What'd she say," I asked automatically.

Pella looked at me and grinned. "She said how come you shut your eyes when I whopped the rabbit."

I glanced down at it, its legs twitching as if it was trying to run. "I guess I don't take kindly to killing." I sounded just like Webb Cotter.

"We're not killing for fun," Athens snapped. "Pa says it's killing each other that's hurtful."

"Are you Quakers too?" Ma and Webb were the only ones I knew of.

Athens knelt down in the grass, slipped the knife from around her neck, cut the snare, and picked up the rabbit. "Nope. Pa says we're Mormons who took a different trail." She turned to face me. "I forgot the other day," she began and then started over. "I meant to tell you that if the loser does pull out the peg with his teeth, he gets the winner's knife to keep." She tossed the knife to me.

I caught it in midair. I figured she'd made up that rule along with all the rest, but I wanted a knife bad enough that I didn't care. I slipped the thong over my head and tucked it inside my shirt.

"Now that we have the rabbit, I'm supposed to ask you to come over and eat with us tomorrow." She didn't wait for an answer. She had all the answers as it was.

After we got back to the soddy and the three of them had left, I sat on the porch trying to think what I could take as a present for their July Christmas. Splinter was playing tag with Dandy until he got tuckered out and curled up in a ball next to the fence. He didn't even raise his head when I brought a pail of water up from the creek. Dandy nickered to me and came dancing as fresh as ever.

Before he stuck his nose in for a drink, he leaned over and nuzzled my neck like he used to do his mare. Maybe he liked the way I smelled. I smoothed his forelock, rubbed his neck, and started thinking that if I was going over to the Masons' for Christmas stew, I'd better take me a bath.

It took a while to find the last of the lye soap Ma had tucked away and then no time at all to get back to the creek, strip down, and give myself a good scrubbing up to and including behind my ears. The water was cold, but the evening was warm so I dried myself with my shirt, wadded everything into a bundle, and started back to the cabin.

Dandy trotted across the lot and edged up to the fence like a dark shadow in the twilight. It was magic—him standing so still, for once, his head turned toward me, his feet not moving.

I dropped my clothes on the ground, climbed up on the fence, took hold of his mane, and slid on to his back as quiet as a tadpole moving in the creek. Then we were flying. I couldn't tell where my skin stopped and his began, but I felt the flow of his muscles and the pounding of his heart as we raced the length of the lot until I went one way and he went the other. Somehow, my trip to the ground seemed to take longer than the ride. It didn't matter because for halfway around the lot, my face against his neck, I had ridden Dandy.

Getting up off the ground hurt for a minute, but by the time I'd crawled through the fence and picked up my clothes, I figured that nothing was broken. Dandy was in the far corner and didn't look like he planned on coming back in my direction. Splinter had waked up and was licking at my legs, and I wasn't sure but what I'd dreamed the whole thing.

Inside the house, I lit a candle, looked at my arm and leg scrubbed raw from the fall, and knew our ride had been real.

In the morning I rummaged through the trunk that held what few clothes I owned till I came up with a pair of britches Ma had made me just before she got sick and a shirt that had belonged to my real father. She'd been saving that for me until I grew, but I figured that even if it was too big at least it wasn't ripped.

I went out and sat down on the porch step. I still didn't have anything to take for a present. The hot wind blew whirligigs of dust across the burned wheat field, and I thought that if I'd been a wheat seed, I wouldn't have sprouted either. The only thing that grew no matter what the weather was the buffalo grass that covered the plains. I wondered what it was that made Webb Cotter so stubborn in picking the worst place in all of Kansas to set up a homestead. Out of the whole one hundred twenty acres, he had only one little field of dead wheat to show for all the work and the money.

Thinking of him made me think of Ma again. I knew as sure as if she whispered in my ear what to take as a present. "The greatest gift is giving freely to someone else what you love." That thing I loved most, next to Dandy, was the only thing I had to give. I hustled back inside the soddy, and pulled Ma's picture out from under my mattress and ran out across the homestead toward the Masons'.

I saw Athens coming to meet me when she was nothing but a speck in the distance. For once, she was by herself. I held the painting behind my back as she got close.

"I was afraid you forgot," she said. She sounded different. Maybe it was because she was wearing a dress.

"I wouldn't forget." The words sounded funny. Athens was easier to talk to when she had on her pa's cast-off britches. "Here," I said, holding out the painted shingle. "It's a present."

She took the shingle, looked at one side, and turned it over.

"It's a picture," I tried to explain.

"Oh! Sure."

"You're holding it upside down," I said, thinking it really wasn't the right gift for Athens after all.

"Oh, now I see." She turned the shingle right side up. "That crazy boy! Look. He's got his arm wrapped around that big old lion!"

"It's called 'Peaceable Kingdom.' " I tried to explain more.

"Poor little kid." Athens shook her head. "Wearing nothing but a sheet out in that jungle. Skeeters'll eat him alive."

"What it says . . ." I went on, even if I didn't think she was hearing me.

She wasn't. "Lions have awful big teeth and so do wolves

37

even if their mouths are shut. Sheep won't hurt him, though."

I kept on trying. "See, those fierce animals are all kneeling with the steer, and the lamb's with this boy in the middle because if lions would quit eating sheep then you could walk through a jungle wearing a sheet and nothing would hurt you."

I'd never put the idea into words before, but I liked how they sounded.

"So," I continued, "if things didn't kill each other, nobody would have to be afraid." Then I felt guilty. "I don't think it means rabbits, though."

I looked down the road, and coming toward us was a stairstep of little straw-haired kids with Topeka's carrottop tagging along last. Together we walked back to their dugout, Athens holding the shingle against her chest. I hoped Ma's homemade paint wouldn't rub off on her dress.

Pella kept busy trying to stop Topeka from eating the blue flowers of the bull thistles. Terry Haute and Normal hung onto each other, looking at me and giggling.

The rabbit stew was mighty thin and there wasn't much meat, but what with my new knife, it was the best Christmas I ever had.

GOING FOR BROKE

Chapter Four

*T*he day after Christmas it took a lot of talking and the last of the molasses before Dandy stood still long enough to let me loop the rope around his neck and drape the seed sack across his back. I hadn't forgotten our late night ride and neither had he. The bouncing he'd given me was just now beginning to hurt. I was stiff and sore and walking like an old man as I led him around the lot, Splinter bounding ahead of us.

"You tried to ride him, didn't you?" Her voice scared all of us. Splinter barked, Dandy snorted, and I almost dropped the rope.

I tried to pretend I'd known she was there, hanging on the fence, all the time. "How do you know?"

"Either you got thrown off a horse or you've got so much starch in your pants that you look stove up." Athens shook her head. "I told you I'd tell you what came next." Then she grinned and asked, "Did it hurt much?"

"It was worth it," I told her, wishing I could explain what being on Dandy's back had felt like. "How come you didn't tell me you'd be here today?"

"I didn't know it until my feet brought me. Do you want to get started teaching him and do it right this time? Maybe if we go slow, just a little bit every day, he won't mind."

Slow is exactly how we went, every day for the next week. Athens came at the same time each morning because, she explained, "It's not so much *what* we do, but it's got to be alike every time we do it. That way Dandy will get used to it."

Her idea was simple, but it worked. He already didn't mind the seed sack on his back as long as it wasn't me and when she had me gather up some prairie grass and stuff it in the bag, it didn't bother him all that much though he looked funny. I'd lead him and Athens walked along beside holding on to the burlap bag so it wouldn't slide off and scare him.

Finally, when we'd stuffed the bag as full as we could, we brought some big stones from the creek and added them to the load. For extra weight, she said, and it didn't bother Dandy one bit. He just danced along between us like he thought he was in a parade.

The only thing that worried me was that the days were slipping away and it wouldn't be long until Webb came back. I didn't care if I did get a whipping afterward, but I wanted to really ride Dandy before I had to pay for it. I had

40

to stick with the lie I'd already told Athens, so all I said was, "If I'm going to surprise Webb, we've got to move faster than this."

She pulled the sack off Dandy's back and looked at me for a long time like she was measuring to see if I'd grown taller. She reminded me of Ma when she'd been making sure I told the truth about really scrubbing my elbows after a Saturday night bath. I wondered if all women could look people straight in the eyes like that. She didn't even blink. "If you're going to break your neck, this is as good a time as any."

I was a little scared, I'll admit. Not so much of getting on Dandy's back as of Athen's watching me come flying off. It's one thing to make a fool of yourself in private; it's another to have somebody watch. At least Pella and Topeka weren't around.

Of course there wasn't any saddle. Webb was using the only one we owned and I didn't think Dandy would have taken to it anyway. And there wasn't any bridle, which was just as well because I *knew* he'd never let me get a bit between his teeth. There was just us—Dandy and me—to do it the best we could.

"What happens first?" I asked. By this time, I was convinced that whether I liked it or not, Athens knew more about the whole business than I did. Besides, something about her made me trust her even after mumblety-peg.

"Bring him up side the fence and let me hold him. Then you climb on the rail and sit still as a tick."

That wasn't hard. We'd taken turns leading Dandy

around, and though I knew he liked me best, he sure didn't have anything against Athens, so I did what she told me.

"Now what?" I asked, balancing on the top rail.

"Just reach out and hold his mane and slip your leg over his back, but don't wiggle and don't clamp your legs around his belly. You're not supposed to be going anywhere. You just want him to get used to your weight. Then I'll lead him while you're sitting there. And remember, don't move."

I knew exactly what was going to happen and if I hadn't remembered, the scabs on my arm and leg would have reminded me. When I slid off the fence and onto Dandy's back, I felt his hide quiver like it did when a fly settled on him, and as I gritted my teeth and closed my eyes waiting for him to set off at full gallop and me to go cartwheeling through the air, I let out a big breath.

"Hold on to his mane," Athens said, sounding like this happened every day, "and don't bounce around up there." She walked away from the fence, the rope in her hand and Dandy right at her side while she talked to him in a voice that was too soft for me to hear the words.

I sat as straight and as quiet as I could, holding my breath again and wondering how long it would take him to pull that rope right out of her hands.

It didn't happen. By the time we reached the end of the lot, turned around, and headed back to where we'd begun, it still hadn't happened, even with Splinter flipping around in front of us like a fool. Dandy wasn't exactly doing what you could call walking—it was more as if he was moving to some kind of music that only he could hear. I couldn't be sure just when he'd move in which direction or with which hoof. Even at that, though he wasn't moving fast, he jarred every sore bone in my body.

When we got back to where we started, Athens said, without looking up at me and talking just a little louder than the voice she'd been using with Dandy, "Now, just slide off as smooth and slick as you can, but keep your hands on him all the way so he'll know what you're doing."

I did and Dandy knew. Athens gave us both a grin and a pat on our shoulders that made me, at least, feel like nothing I could ever do again would be half as important as what we'd done that day. I felt like hugging her the way I used to hug Ma, but my arms just couldn't make the right shape so I settled for a spit handshake.

At first it was enough to be able to sit on Dandy's back while Athens led us around the lot, but after two or three days, I wanted more. The only problem was that without a bridle there wasn't anything I could do.

Athens must have guessed how I was feeling because the next time she showed up, she brought a present with her. Of course, when she handed it to me, I thought it was nothing more than a coil of old, frayed rope. "What did you bring this for?" I asked. "I don't need a lasso. Dandy's not going to be a cow pony, he's going to be a riding horse."

She looked at me with eyes all squinched up like she was peering inside my head and not finding anything there. "Caleb, sometimes you got no more brains than Topeka. Don't you even know a hackamore when you see one?"

Truth was, I didn't know what she was talking about and

I owned up to it. I'd found out that telling her the truth saved us a lot of time.

"See," she said, grabbing it back and shaking the coil out, "you put this part over Dandy's nose. Look here, it's a slipknot, and these are the reins. When you pull on them," she talked slow and loud like I was hard of hearing, "the knot tightens and you can make him go where you want to."

That's when I knew it was a present every bit as special as the knife she'd given me. With the hackamore, if I could stay on Dandy's back, I could ride him any time I wanted to. I wouldn't have to wait for Athens to show up. I was so excited that I forgot to thank her. I wasn't sure what Dandy would think so I held it out and let him sniff it. He tried nibbling, but when he found out it wasn't sweet, he wasn't much interested.

"Just slip it on real easy while you talk to him and don't pull it tight till you're on his back."

Dandy didn't much like the feel of the rope around his nose from the way he shook his head and stomped, but he didn't jerk away.

Athens had said that if I could convince Dandy that I'd never do anything to hurt him, he'd do anything I asked. Hoping she was right, I got up on his back holding the rope reins in one hand.

"Remember to squeeze him with your legs and don't stick your heels in his sides." She sounded as out of breath as I felt.

I took a rein in each hand, closed my eyes and gently squeezed Dandy's ribs. I didn't open my eyes until I felt him start to move away from the fence. He didn't exactly walk, but then he never did. At least he didn't take off at a run and when I pulled on the right rein, he turned like we'd been doing it all our lives. Halfway down the fence line, I squeezed a little harder and he broke into a trot that had me bouncing around worse than the seed sacks ever did.

"Quit squeezing and pull back slow with both hands!" Athens shouted.

I don't know who was more surprised—me or Dandy. We both stopped at the same time and in the same place. I didn't figure either of us was ready for any lessons in backing up and I was plain scared to ask him to go faster, so I settled for walking and trotting until Athens stopped us.

"I have to go home now," she said.

I pulled up to the fence and slid off Dandy as smooth as I could manage. "Do you have to take the hackamore back?" Then I felt bad because it sounded like I didn't care whether she stayed or went.

She understood, though, cause she didn't get mad. "Nope, you can keep it. Pa doesn't even know it's gone. You can use it as long as you need it." She didn't wait for an answer.

After she left, I pulled the rope off Dandy and rubbed the spot where it had circled his nose. He let me hold his head between my hands and press my cheek against his forehead. "Oh, Dandy," I whispered, sure he understood. "Now we can go anywhere. It'll always be like this—just you and me. Nothing will ever change." He answered with the soft nicker he always used for me, leaned down, and started cropping the short grass.

The next weeks went faster than any other time in my life. I spent all day most every day with Dandy and I paid as much attention to grooming him as I did to riding him around the lot. He liked to be curried and he'd stand almost still while I worked on his mane and tail until I could run my fingers through them and never find a single tangle. He even got so he'd let me pick up his hooves and clean out the dry clods of dirt that sometimes got caught there.

Athens came and sat on the fence to watch us and sometimes she brought Pella and Topeka. That worried me at first because I was afraid they'd go home and blab to their folks, but Athens said not to worry. "Pella won't tell because she knows I'll beat her up if she does and it doesn't matter about Topeka because nobody understands her anyway."

The next day was too hot to do anything but stay in the shade, me and Dandy together drowsing through the afternoon. Even Splinter gave up on chasing rabbits and flopped down beside us out of the sun. Athens hadn't showed up so I figured she and her family were trying to keep cool inside their dugout. Along toward evening, a breeze started up, enough to stir Dandy's mane and rouse Splinter out of his sleep. He stuck his nose in the air and sniffed like he could taste the wind, then took off like a gunshot. Dandy whinnied like he always did when the dog left for a run.

Without thinking long enough to get scared, I fetched the hackamore, slipped it over Dandy's nose, and got on his back. When I unlatched the gate there was nothing between us and the sunset but grass. I leaned forward and tried to keep the shaking out of my voice. "Come on, boy, let's go find Splinter." I took a good grip on the reins and squeezed with my legs.

One minute we were standing still and the next we were moving so fast that the wind blurred my eyes. Dandy didn't bother with a trot. He broke into a flat-out gallop, and by the time my vision cleared I knew without looking that the soddy was far behind us. I wasn't sure if I could stop him and I didn't want to try. I felt and heard the pounding of his hooves, and, crouched over his neck, I hung tight as the burrs in Splinter's coat.

We caught up with the dog and passed him, and still we ran. I didn't know how far we'd gone when Dandy began to slow, first to a canter, then to a trot and finally, as I pulled on the reins, to his dancing walk.

After that first ride away from the homestead out into the freedom of the prairie, I couldn't see any good reason for us to stay penned up in the lot and the more I rode Dandy, the more sure I was that he'd do anything I'd ask except stand still for very long. Maybe he wasn't what Webb Cotter would call broke, but he turned and he stopped when I wanted him to, and that was good enough for me.

I didn't count on seeing Athens for a while. The whole family had come down with something called chicken pox—an itchy kind of sickness that Mason caught first in one of his visits to Fort Larned. Athens was just coming down with it the last time I saw her and while I felt sorry for her, what with the red rash and all, she was so disagreeable she wasn't any fun to be around anyway.

My favorite time to ride was in the evening just an hour or so before sunset, kind of because it was the lonesomest part of the day and mostly because when we turned around and headed back, the whole world was like the colors in Ma's painting. And even if there weren't any lions or sheep or steers, there was every other kind of animal—herds of buffalo that looked like dark hills against the horizon, whole cities of prairie dogs, and antelopes that dashed past us even faster than Dandy could run.

I owned everything I could see. It must have been sort of the way God felt in Genesis after He created the world.

Only trouble was He created it too hot on Kansas afternoons, so one day when I woke early and the sun was just busting into the sky and the morning breeze hadn't turned into a wind yet, I called Splinter, put the hackamore on Dandy, and we started out in a new direction.

We headed northwest toward Fort Hays.

As always, Splinter took off in a dead run like he had to meet someone very important and was already a day late. It was all I could do to hold Dandy to a trot—I wasn't in any hurry and I wanted to keep a close eye on what few landmarks there were so I could find our way back.

I never could figure out why people, white people, came here when there were so many other places to be. Me, I didn't have a choice any more than Splinter and Dandy. But folks like the Masons—out of all those states they'd lived in—they just kept pushing on. I was so busy trying to puzzle it out that I didn't notice Splinter until we were almost on top of him.

He was coming toward us, not running, but limping on three legs, one paw held in the air like he was trying to wave. I almost laughed until he lay down, whimpered, and started licking his foot. He looked so miserable that without thinking, I stopped Dandy and slid down off his back. As soon as I did it, I knew how dumb I was. How could I get back up again? The only way I'd ever managed to get on Dandy was from the top of the rail fence.

I tucked the rope reins under my arm and hoped Dandy was as interested in Splinter as I was. When I picked up his paw, it didn't take long to see what was the matter. A barb from a cactus had gone clear through. No wonder he was limping. It was a mean thing, over two inches long, and when I tried to pull it free, it wouldn't come. Nothing to do but cut it loose if I could manage and if Splinter would let me, but I couldn't do it and hold Dandy at the same time.

That's when I did something even dumber than getting on the ground in the first place. I knotted the ends of the reins around my waist so both my hands were free and slipped the leather thong over my head and opened my knife. It only took a few minutes but it must have seemed a whole lot longer to Splinter before I managed to cut off the barb and slide the thorn out of his paw.

When Splinter started barking, I thought he was trying to thank me. When Dandy whinnied, I thought he was tired of standing still. When I looked up, I saw them.

Cheyennes! I could tell right away because Webb had explained how they painted themselves. Twelve of them on horseback sat watching me from the top of a small rise.

I just had time to untie the reins from my waist and stand up before they were all around me. I was too surprised to be scared. They didn't have any weapons drawn and they weren't yelling or anything, but when they got really close so I could see their faces I closed my eyes and swallowed hard trying to pretend it wasn't really happening.

Before I could move again, one of them, a boy not much older than me, slid off his buckskin pony and ran toward me. I clenched my fists thinking I might try to make a fight of it, but it wasn't me he was interested in.

With a shout, he grabbed a handful of mane and vaulted onto Dandy's back like he'd been shot from a bow. Dandy reared and the boy was on the ground even faster than he'd got off it. If things hadn't been like they were I might have laughed, but as it was I had a hard time breathing. They didn't care about me one way or the other. They were going to steal Dandy and there was nothing I could do about it.

I tried anyway. If they were going to kill and scalp me, it didn't make much difference what I said, so I yelled one of the few Cheyenne words I knew, "Horse!" and then I pointed to me. Webb Cotter said sign language worked and I sure was willing to try it.

The men on horseback laughed, the boy glared at me and tried the same thing again. This time Dandy didn't wait to feel anything on his back. As soon as the hands touched his mane, he lashed out with both back legs, straightened, and bucked like he was going to bust himself in two.

The boy landed hard right beside me, almost near enough to touch. The Cheyennes laughed again and called out words I couldn't understand, but I knew they were making fun of him.

Dandy had yanked the reins free of my hands the first time he reared, and I couldn't understand why he hadn't taken off running the way Splinter had a little earlier. Instead, he moved closer to me, doing his standing-still dance and nudged me with his nose like he was asking me to think of some way to get us out of this mess. I didn't have a single thought in my head.

The boy got to his feet and stood for a minute catching his breath. I couldn't help but think that with his moccasins, leather pants, and a golden eagle feather hanging around his neck, he had better clothes than I did. He was just about ready to take one more try at Dandy when one of the older men rode up, grabbed the dangling reins, and looked down at me like some judge straight out of Webb Cotter's Old Testament.

He reeled off a whole bunch of words, but I only understood a few of them—"Hawk" and he pointed toward the boy beside me. Then the word for horse. After that, he pointed toward the boy's pony, then toward Dandy. All the time, the men behind him were talking among themselves, nodding and shouting out things. If they hadn't been Cheyennes and we hadn't been out in the middle of Kansas with no one else around for miles, it might have seemed like some kind of Saturday afternoon get-together.

The difference was that if they wanted to they could kill me and take Dandy and no one, not even Webb Cotter, would guess what happened. That's when my knees started to shake.

I looked over at Hawk and made the hand motion for "I don't understand," not thinking he'd bother to sign back, but he did and he didn't seem to be mad about having been laughed at. He didn't look like he wanted to ask me to join up with the tribe either.

Our trying to understand each other took a while and Dandy was getting as restless as the Indian ponies, but I finally understood what was going on. It would be a race between me on Dandy and the boy, Hawk, on his buckskin. Whoever won kept both horses. I didn't ask what else happened to the loser. I didn't have much choice. They could have killed me in a minute if they'd wanted to. They still could. My biggest problem right away was how to get back up on Dandy. I sure had no intention of trying Hawk's way because I knew I wouldn't fare a bit better than he had. It hurt my pride but I couldn't figure out any other way, so with a lot of motions and pointing by me, the boy under-stood and gave me a boost up. That's when I really heard laughter. Still, it was better than arrows.

Some of the men lined up in one place where we were supposed to start, and the rest rode out a ways, and that, I figured, was the finish. I knew how fast Dandy could run—if he'd just do it in a straight line—but Hawk's pony looked strong and sleek from living off summer grass.

The brave who'd talked to me held a lance in his hand and when he brought it down, I pointed Dandy in the right direction, dug my heels in his flanks, and yelled in his ears. I don't know what I said but it must have worked because by the time we got to that other bunch of Indians we were far in front of Hawk.

I managed to get Dandy slowed and was thinking of riding straight back to the homestead, when Hawk, instead of stopping, whirled his buckskin and headed full speed back the way he'd come. That's when I knew the race wasn't over.

We started out behind and I wasn't sure we could catch up, except I'd forgotten that Dandy never could stand any-thing moving ahead of him whether it was Splinter or an antelope or even a speedy Kansas jackrabbit. We were right up beside Hawk when I felt Dandy push forward like he'd only been playing at running before and by the time I finally got him stopped I was as much out of breath as he was.

The Cheyennes caught up with us before I could turn Dandy around, and this time they were yelling, waving bows, and couldn't have looked more fierce if they'd been on the war trail. Mostly I hoped that they really did kill people before they scalped them.

They made a bigger circle around us than before, and just when I thought they'd all turn me into a pincushion like the one Ma used to have in her sewing box, Hawk got off his pony and led it up to me.

That's when my eyes started watering and my legs started shaking again even if my feet weren't on the ground. Somehow I thought how I'd feel if things had been turned around—and how Hawk felt giving up his pony just because he'd lost a race he'd been shoved into.

So I looked at him, shook my head, and tried my hardest to show through signs and my few Cheyenne words that his pony belonged to him like Dandy belonged to me. I had to do it twice because I was bad at shaping words with my hands.

I heard the men talking with each other, a rumbling sound with a shout now and then. Finally the leader called something to Hawk. It didn't sound like an order, more like a question. The boy nodded and looked up at me.

He spoke in words I didn't understand, but his voice was clear. Then, he reached for the eagle feather, pulled the thong that held it over his head, and gave it to me.

As I took it from him, our hands touched and before I had time to think, I grabbed the leather thong that held my knife, lifted it from my neck, and offered it to him. He took it and nodded, his eyes so dark I thought I could see my reflection in them. I didn't know any words to say, so I made the sign for *friend*.

I glanced back once as Dandy and I began our ride toward the homestead. The Cheyennes had disappeared. Nothing was behind us except an endless, empty land.

THE SELLOUT

Chapter Five

The wind blew all the time in Kansas: winter, fall, spring, and most of the summer. Ma asked Webb once, "Doesn't it ever stop?"

"I'll plant a windbreak," Webb promised, but the wind broke down the trees before they could break the wind.

A person would think a good Kansas wind would blow up a little rain once in a while, but that summer was so dry that when Webb Cotter got back from his work on the Santa Fe Trail with the winter wheat seed he'd bought with the little money he'd earned, there wasn't any hope of replanting. The whole earth was drying up. Cracks spiraled across the wheat field and even the buffalo grass was brittle.

"Don't know what to do. Can't sell out. Nobody to buy the place."

We were sitting on the porch steps, the sun hanging on the horizon blurring the sky in shimmering heat waves. I thought Webb was talking to me, but he could have been just putting words together to see if they made as much sense as what he was thinking.

"Mason's pulling up stakes. Going back to Topeka. Says out here's no place to raise a family. He thinks the Indians ought to have the land."

Athens hadn't told me they were moving. I hadn't seen her for days because Webb kept me busy hoeing weeds that grew even when everything else died. Maybe, though, it had been too hot for her to walk over.

The sun was down, an ugly red glow stretching halfway across the sky. I leaned against the sod house, tipping my head back so I could swallow the salty taste in my throat.

"There's something about land . . . about working it and caring for it . . . having something to pass on." Webb stared at the dead crops like he could change them to green if he looked hard enough.

If he was talking about saving anything for me, he needn't have bothered. I wasn't planning on grubbing out a homestead. When I got old enough I'd join the cavalry like my pa did. I'd wear a uniform and ride Dandy in parades.

"Might could sell the breaking plow," Webb went on, rubbing his fingers through his hair.

I quit listening. I hated homesteading. I hated living with Webb Cotter. I hated Athens for leaving.

Days were lonely when she didn't come running across the prairie or when I didn't sneak off to meet her. We spent afternoons on the bank of the creek talking about the world and life and things deep and mysterious, things I'd never dared think about before—like ghosts and demons and vampires. Not that I saw her every day, but I always knew that if I didn't see her one day, I'd probably see her the next. Now that she was leaving, I wouldn't have anything to look forward to.

I waited until Webb went to bed, then I walked on down to the lot where Dandy was a black smudge of shadow against the dark sky. He blew a soft, rumbling snort and I stroked his neck, a mass of swirls for those first months after he was born, but now sleek and silky as the inside of a milkweed pod. He danced to one side, then turned and nuzzled me, wind ruffling his thick mane.

Athens had tried to convince me that once horses used to have five toes on their front feet and three on their back ones, but they had to run so fast to escape dinosaurs that they lost all but one toe on each foot. She said a hoof was just one big toenail and that's why it had to be trimmed. I didn't believe her for a minute, but I was going to miss her even if she did make up things.

She even tried to make me believe Dandy had four more teeth than the mare, but we couldn't get him to stand still long enough to count. I was going to ask her how come horses could sleep standing up, but it didn't look like I'd ever have the chance.

The night grew darker, the prairie emptier, the Kansas wind wilder. I crept back to the house but I couldn't sleep. I stared into the blackness until the dim light of another morning outlined the square of the window, and then I closed my eyes.

When I woke up and went outside that day, Dandy wasn't waiting for me in the lot. My insides felt like somebody had yanked them plumb out because my first notion was that he'd been stolen. I knew he couldn't have broken the fence and run off, because the cow pony was still there dozing in the early sun.

I tried to work up enough wet for whistling, but before I could manage, Dandy whinnied from the barn. I ran toward it wondering if he'd got hurt somehow and if Webb had put him in for doctoring.

When I opened the door Webb was standing with his hand on Dandy's withers. "Is he all right?" I asked.

"He's fine." He frowned across Dandy's back, then glanced away like he wished I'd disappear. "Makes it by a finger."

"Makes what?"

"They're buying horses up at Fort Hays. Wanted to tell you last evening, but. . . ."

My mouth was full of words that wouldn't come out.

"Anyhow, he just makes the size limit. I measured."

"He's only a two-year-old!" Suddenly I was shouting.

"They want young horses." He still wasn't looking at me.

My mouth had the same bitter taste as when he'd told me Ma was dead. He hadn't been able to look me in the eyes then either.

"You can't sell him. Not to the army."

Webb smoothed Dandy's mane. "It's sell him or lose this place. Should have money left over to breed the mare again."

"He's not broke to ride." Webb Cotter never had found out what I'd done while he was away and I didn't mind lying.

"Halter broke is fine. They'll do the rest."

My stomach began to cramp. I grabbed a pitchfork, ran out behind the barn, and shoved it into the ground over and over until I ran out of muscle. I didn't think I was crying until the sky was a blurry blue and the dead wheat a shimmering sheet of brown.

I stared until I remembered what Ma told me: "Look up, Caleb. You can't cry tears with your head up."

I wiped my nose against my shirt sleeve and started back to the barn. Webb didn't know it, but if he planned on selling Dandy, he'd have to catch us first. The minute there was a chance, the two of us would ride off even if it meant heading straight south into the Indian Territory. I wasn't sure how I'd manage, but the notion took hold of my mind like a noose around a rabbit's neck.

Webb was still in the barn. "You don't think I *want* to sell him, do you?"

"I don't know," I mumbled, trying not to look at him.

"It's down to this. He's the only thing we got that any-one'll buy. Could say we're dirt poor."

I propped the pitchfork against the wall and didn't an-swer.

For once he looked straight at me so I had to look at him. "You weren't thinking I was selling him to be a war horse, did you?"

"That's what you said, wasn't it?"

"No, I didn't. Word is that Custer, he's head of the Seventh Cavalry, wants a horse for his wife. A saddle horse."

"Is someone coming to look at Dandy?"

"I'll be taking him to the fort tomorrow. The sale's Wednesday and I want him fresh." He wasn't talking to me; he'd forgotten I was there. "Thirty miles won't be a hard ride."

I didn't stay to hear what else he was thinking. I had plans to make, even if I wasn't sure what they were. Mostly, though, I wanted to get as far away from Webb Cotter as I could.

Late that afternoon I was getting rid of what was left of our dried-up garden, piling dead squash vines in a heap for burning when Athens came running across our lot, clearing the rail fence with a one-handed vault that would have put any boy to shame and sending Splinter into a barking fit.

"Pa says you're selling Dandy to the cavalry!" she said, gasping for breath.

"I'm not selling him. Webb is." I yanked at the vines that lay like rope under the dry leaves, mad that everyone, even Dandy, was going and I was supposed to be left behind in a place I never wanted to be anyway.

Usually I didn't have to worry about talking when Athens was around, but now she was quiet and I couldn't think of anything to say.

Finally, in a soft voice that didn't even sound like hers,

she said, "We're leaving tomorrow. I wanted to say good-bye to Dandy." She started back toward the lot. "Is Webb going to breed the mare again?"

I stuck my pitchfork into the pile of weeds and vines. "I'm not staying to find out."

She came back toward me. "What are you going to do, Caleb?" Her eyes, blue-flecked with green, reminded me of Ma's—not so much the color as the way they looked when she said my name. It was funny how nice my name sounded when Athens said it.

I straightened up and walked over to the fence, propped my foot on the bottom rail, and looked across the homestead—dry and brown as if it was winter. "Dandy and me are lighting out tonight," I explained as if I had it all planned out.

"You're running away?" She wasn't looking at me. She was on her knees petting Splinter, which seemed kind of funny because she'd never paid him much mind before.

"Not running! *Riding*," I said, trying to make a joke. Hearing her words scared me.

"You can't. You wouldn't have anywhere to go. Besides, Webb would catch up with you in two minutes." She stood and faced me.

She was right about that. I tried another idea that made more sense.

"Then I'll follow Dandy tomorrow. I'll enlist in Custer's Seventh Cavalry!"

"You can't. You're not big enough."

"I'll walk tall. And if they still won't take me, I'll just tag along." I was sure that would work. Here I was arguing with her when I knew she'd come to say good-bye. I guess losing her and Dandy all at the same time was more than I could handle.

Maybe she felt as bad as I did because she never got around to saying "so long" or "I'll miss you" or whatever people say when they're losing something. Instead, she whispered to me even if there wasn't anyone else around, "I won't tell anyone ever, Caleb. About you riding Dandy."

She spit on her palm and held out her hand. I did the same, and we shook for the last time. I watched her walk away until she melted clean out of sight.

I was tuckered out with good-byes. Maybe Athens was too.

It crossed my mind to feel bad about leaving Webb. I couldn't tell him what I was going to do because he'd stop me, and I couldn't leave a note because he didn't know how to read. Still, I didn't feel quite right sitting there with him that night and pretending it was just like any other time.

He must have, for once, felt kind of the same, because instead of staring at the empty fields like he usually did before bedtime, he made a stab at talking. Neither one of us was used to it, so it didn't get far.

"Mason's bringing the mare back tomorrow afternoon. Bought a mule to take them east." He leaned against the side of the soddy, kicking up little whorls of dust with the toe of his boot.

It took me a while to think of something to answer. "We could go, too," I finally said.

"You may not understand now," he turned so he was facing me, "but this place belongs to us. It's all there is. We just got to wait it through. Like the Bible says, these are the lean years. The fat ones will come."

"Not if it doesn't rain," I answered, but not like I was trying to go against what he said.

Skinny or lardy, all those years weren't worth waiting around for. The more I thought about what I'd told Athens about joining the cavalry, the better it sounded. Not that I was interested in fighting, but there wasn't any war going on anyway. I'd sign up and Dandy would be my horse. We'd get a free saddle and a chance to hear bands play and march in parades like the one I'd seen back in Fort Leavenworth before I ever heard of Webb Cotter.

"For everything there is a season." His voice was low. "Ecclesiastes, chapter three, verse one."

I thought he was going to tell me to fetch the Bible and read it to him, but it was too dark by that time.

"What do you want me to do while you're gone?" I tried to keep the lie out of my voice and I was glad he couldn't see my face. Ma always knew when I wasn't being truthful, and Webb had gotten pretty good at guessing.

That made things easier right away because if there was one thing Webb could do quick, it was make a list of chores even if he had to invent them. This one started with "Clean the mare. She'll probably need a currying," and ended with "Finish clearing up the garden."

I almost said "Yes, sir" sort of practicing for the cavalry, but changed it to what I usually said, "Yeah."

By that time we'd run out of sentences, so I wasn't sorry to hear Webb say, "Guess I'll get to bed. Going to be a hard day tomorrow for both of us."

I couldn't see what was going to be so hard for him sitting on his pony and dragging my Dandy along behind him. As for me, he was right. It would be a long thirty miles to Fort Hays, but my feet were already itching to move.

I thought Webb would be starting out for the fort about midmorning, since he had plenty of time to get there, but that next day when I woke and looked out, the cow pony stood saddled beside the rail fence, his head down. I pulled on some clothes and ran out the door. Webb came from the barn leading a frisky Dandy wearing the mare's old leather halter.

"Tie up Splinter so he don't follow."

I couldn't bear to look at Dandy and I couldn't stand to look at Webb. "Maybe he won't sell."

"He'll sell." Webb slipped a foot into the stirrup and swung into the saddle. "And remember maybe in the spring we'll breed the mare again." The cow pony moved out. The lead rope tightened. Dandy tossed his head to free himself.

"Come on now. Settle down," Webb shouted. Splinter barked, standing on his hind legs straining to follow.

Dandy reared back but the rope pulled him down. He trotted out ahead and another jerk pulled him back. He danced sideways and the tug came again, yanking his head into the flank of the cow pony. I stood, my arms hugging the weathered porch post, watching until they were out of sight.

Inside the cabin, I grabbed the bundle I'd made the night before—an extra pair of pants and a sweater Ma'd knit for me the winter before she died. I wore everything else I owned and carried my boots. I had only one pair that fit and figured I'd save them until later; besides, the bottoms of my feet were almost as tough as leather anyway.

I crossed our dried wheat field on a dead run, and by the time I reached the wagon trail, Webb and Dandy were gone so I settled into a fast walk. I had hoofprints to guide me and I wasn't afraid of getting lost. I tried not to think of Splinter, tied up until Webb got back, or of Athens going away. I wondered what Webb would do when he discovered he didn't have me to boss around or read the Bible for him.

About the middle of the morning, my feet began to burn, my legs ached, and my back felt like I'd been toting a hundred-pound sack of wheat. By the time the sun was overhead, I'd stripped off my extra shirt and tied it, along with my boots, into my bundle. I sat beside the trail to rest a spell. That's when I remembered I'd forgotten to bring food.

From the looks of the sun when I woke up, it was the middle of the afternoon. I saw a fringe of trees far ahead and that meant a river or at least a stream, so I took out cross-country. It was an hour before I reached the river, and when I got there, I plunged my feet into the cool water before drinking until my stomach squished when I stood up.

I thought about finding a log and floating to the fort, only the water wasn't deep enough. There was nothing to do but go back to the trail, but I was tired and so hungry I almost gave up. Except for a strip of slippery elm, I hadn't eaten anything since the night before. Slippery elm mushes up when you chew it so you think you're eating something even when you're not.

It was growing dark, and I found a big cottonwood tree with bushes around the trunk, so I snuggled in there, using my bundle for a pillow. The water made a soft sound, and with the leaves sifting the breeze over me, I pretended I was in Ma's peaceable kingdom.

The morning was so cold that I shivered myself awake, pulled on some of the clothes I'd pulled off the day before, and started back to the trail. I hadn't clipped off more than a mile or so when I heard the creak and rattle of a wagon coming up behind me.

The first thing I thought was that Athens must have told after all and it was Mason come to fetch me back. Wagons on our part of the plains were about as rare as a windless day.

When the rig pulled up next to me, the driver looked as surprised by me as I was by him.

"You lost or loco?" The man's voice was bigger than he was. He was perched high above a load of more buffalo skins than I'd ever seen.

"I'm headed for Hays," I answered, trying to make something that looked crazy seem ordinary.

"Want a ride or are you going to wait for a train to come along?" He laughed at his joke.

"I'll take the ride," I said, climbing up beside him.

He gave the reins a flip and we started moving. "Headed for the horse sale?"

I studied him for a minute out of the corner of my eye. It was hard to see much, what with his full beard, bushy hair, and felt hat pulled low. "Yep," I answered, hoping I sounded older than I felt.

"Don't look like you're selling nothing or you'd be riding it. Not often I run across somebody going for a walk in Indian country." He stuck a chaw of tobacco in his mouth and went on talking. "No sir, here I've drove all the way up from Dodge and not seen a soul except for Kiowas, and there you are out for a weekday stroll."

I thought if I asked him a question he'd forget about asking his own. "You a buffalo hunter?"

"Naw, I let my partners do the shooting. I haul the hides up to the railroad at Hays. I can sell them as fast as they kill them. Your average buffalo isn't too smart." He leaned toward me. "So you were walking all the way to Hays just to look at the horses?"

I didn't want to tell him anything, but I didn't want to

be unfriendly either, so I said, "Thought I might get to see General Custer. I've never seen a real general. He'll be there, won't he?"

"He'll be there, but you're not going to see a *real* general. He's Colonel Custer. Seems he likes folks to *call* him General." The man laughed. "They're not just buying up mounts for the cavalry. He needs himself another horse." He turned to spit a mouthful of tobacco juice over the side of the wagon. "See, the colonel was out after an old bull buffalo not long ago and the way I heard it, he was riding his wife's horse, Custis Lee, but he got excited and shot the horse instead of the buffalo." He spit again.

"What did he do then?" Webb said a man was crazy to be caught on the open plains without a horse.

"According to Custer, if you can believe him, he stared down that old bull until it turned and went loping off to where it came from, Custer's hunting dogs chasing behind. Hour or so later, some cavalry showed up and took the colonel back to camp and that's why he needs a new mount—for his wife." He turned and looked at me. "You from around here?"

The man was full of questions, but hadn't asked my name. "From back south a piece."

"How old are you?"

I did lie then. "Sixteen."

"Pretty scrawny for sixteen. That reminds me—reach down under the seat. The wife put up some vittles and you look like you could use a little meat on your bones."

Vittles might just as well have been a Sunday dinner. Fresh baked bread with slabs of buffalo meat and a slice of apple pie, which we split. That, along with the sun beating down on my layers of clothes and the rhythmic clop of the horses' hooves, made me sleepy. It didn't have the same effect on my new friend. The food opened up a gully-gusher flood of stories.

"You might be able to see Mrs. Custer too. Libbie, he calls her. She's a looker—slim as a whip, hair the color of chestnuts, and a pretty face; a real lady, they say. She'll probably be right out there with the Boy Wonder. She knows horses."

That made me think of Athens and how she'd like to have seen a famous man like Custer and a lady like his wife. Well, maybe she wouldn't. Athens could be real contrary sometimes.

Hays had a main street and that was about all. The place smelled of horses.

"Where you want me to drop you off?"

I didn't know so I said, "Where they're selling the horses."

"At the fort over there—across Big Creek. See?" He pointed ahead where a city of tents and a row of houses stood on a hill.

I hopped down and thanked him for the ride and food before he drove on. By the time I waded the creek, I was sure I was the only one in Kansas who didn't have a mount to sell. Horses of all ages, breeds separated by color, were penned in lots behind what I figured must be the stables. The queer thing was, there didn't seem to be anybody around looking to buy or sell.

I ran to one lot, climbed up on the fence searching for Dandy, but all I could see were the backs of over fifty bay horses. I got down and circled to where a gate separated them from the biggest, longest barn I'd ever seen.

"Looking for something?" I hadn't noticed a man leaning against the barn door.

"When are they going to start selling?"

"Sale's over. It finished up a couple of hours ago."

A soldier on a gray horse cantered up and reined in beside us. "Orders for you, Burke. General will inspect bays in an hour. He says to pick out four or five of the best and bring them to his quarters."

"Sure." Burke yawned and wiped his eyes with the back of his hand.

"In an hour," the soldier repeated. "Custer's wife wants to look at them."

"I heard." Burke answered, still leaning against the barn. He waited until the soldier and horse had disappeared before he went into the building and finally emerged with an armful of halters and a lasso. "Make yourself useful, boy," he said, crawling through the fence and walking to the edge of the milling horses.

I watched as he sent the rope whirling into the herd to settle over the head of a big bay that stood at least two hands taller than Dandy.

"Open the gate," he ordered, as he slipped a halter on the horse's head.

"Right," I shouted back.

Four times he flipped the lasso and four times he repeated, "Get the gate!" and four times I got the gate. After he had the horses tied up to hitching posts, I walked up beside him. "Just one more in here I want, but he's staying clear. See him over there?"

I looked where he was pointing.

It was Dandy!

"I'll get him." I put two fingers in my mouth and let out a whistle that would rattle your eardrums. Dandy turned, ears forward, and started toward me dancing and pushing and nipping and nosing his way through the herd. When he reached me, he stuck his nose in my shoulder so all I could do was bury my face in his mane and wrap my arms around his neck. He didn't come for molasses. He came for *me*.

"Belonged to you, did he?" Burke asked, as he fastened the halter.

"Yes, sir." It was the truth. Dandy did belong to me even if I didn't own him, but I didn't think Burke would understand. He might have been Webb's brother, the way he grunted out words, his face scowling. I didn't think he heard me but I went on anyway. "My stepfather had to sell him to buy seed. He's a homesteader."

Burke did look at me then as I led Dandy up to the other horses. "Rough business, homesteading?"

"Yeah."

"Lonesome, too."

"Yeah."

"Gotta get these over to Custer. I'll manage the four. You bring this one. Has he got a name?"

"Dandy."

Burke stroked the thick black mustache that drooped over the corners of his mouth. "He is that—a dandy. Doesn't he ever stand still?"

"Only when I pet him." I rubbed my hand across his chest. "Maybe. . . ." I began, not wanting to push my luck. "Maybe if I had a currycomb, I could clean him."

Burke didn't answer right away. Instead he tugged at his mustache and looked at us, his eyes black beads under bushy eyebrows. I didn't know which of us he was sizing up. Finally he grunted. "Inside on the bench by the door."

I worked on Dandy, currying and brushing, until he shone like sumac leaves brightened by frost. By the time I finished, what with wearing two shirts and the sun beating down on me, I looked worse than Dandy before his grooming.

"Anyplace I could get clean?" I asked Burke who didn't look as if he was in a hurry to go anywhere. "Maybe I could change my clothes before we go."

"You brought a change of clothes?"

I pointed to the bundle I'd dropped by the fence.

He shook his head and without saying a word, nodded toward the barn.

I might not have looked better, but I felt better without the sweat and dust, and with my hair slicked down. Then I remembered Webb. All I could hope was that he started home as soon as he felt the money in his hands. If he saw me leading Dandy, he'd like as not drag me home. I was about ready to tell Burke that I couldn't go with him when I thought of Ma. She had a way of slipping into my mind at the oddest times.

She'd said that we all had a kind of light inside that, if we were quiet, it'd show us the right thing to do. I don't think my light ever got lit until just then when I knew, Webb Cotter or not, nothing was going to stop me from being with Dandy.

We started toward the wooden houses, Burke with four horses that he didn't have any trouble controlling, and me with Dandy who pranced like he thought he'd won a prize.

"Stop showing off," I muttered. "Act nice! Mrs. Custer might like you if you quit dancing around. Act like you're fit for a lady to ride." He poked me with his nose and kept on taking two steps one way and then three steps the other, kicking up little clouds of dust. It was like Ma said: "You can't change people, you take them as they are." Maybe that was true of horses, too.

We turned a corner leading up to a row of houses all stuck together with a porch running in front. You could have put half a dozen of our soddies in them and still had room left over. Sitting with his boots propped against the railing was a man in fringed buckskins and a broad-brimmed hat cocked at an angle over curly yellow hair and beside him a woman almost as pretty as my mother.

Burke stopped right in front and I led Dandy up. The lady looked down the line of horses and when she saw Dandy and me she smiled. I smiled back because I couldn't help it.

"What do you think, Libbie?" Custer was looking at her, not at us.

"Oh, Autie." Her voice was almost as pretty as her face. "He's gorgeous. The one with the boy."

At the sound of the words, Dandy, as if he knew she was talking about him, arched his neck and did another of his skittery side steps.

I decided right then, thinking of her smile, that if I couldn't have Dandy all to myself, I wouldn't mind sharing him with the colonel's lady.

DANDY'S BOY

Chapter Six

When we got the horses back to the barns, Burke nodded toward the stable door. "Put that Dandy of yours in the second stall next to Old Vic and water him."

"Yes, sir," I answered, coming down hard on the "sir."

"And when you're through, get your duds and come back here. I want to talk to you."

"Yes, sir," I answered again. I almost felt like saluting.

Old Vic was a big sleek bay that stretched her neck and glared at Dandy and me, her nostrils flaring. I hurried us past to the next stall.

"Talk about luck, Dandy. We've got it." The place was at least a hundred times bigger than our lean-to at home and it had clean yellow straw underfoot, a manger full of sweet timothy hay that must have been shipped in by railroad, and smooth-planed boards lining the sides.

"You know what this means?" I went on as I tied him up and brushed my hand across the soft velvet of his nose. "All you have to do is act nice and walk around with the most beautiful lady you've ever seen on your back."

Dandy wasn't paying any attention. He had his mouth full of hay and was munching dreamily as if he couldn't believe what he was eating. The barn smelled sweet with the mixture of leather and horses and sun-cured hay. I gave Dandy a slap on the rump and started for the door. Burke was waiting for me.

"You want a job?"

My mouth opened and I couldn't move a muscle to shut it again.

"Plenty of work around here to do, let alone take care of Mrs. Custer's horse. Pay you a going wage and you bunk in the stable with the rest of us."

I took a big breath getting ready to answer and waited for him to ask about where I came from and who my folks were, but he went on as if he had to talk me into saying yes when all I was trying to do was get my mouth fixed so I could say it.

"You mean I can take care of Dandy?"

"That's why you're being hired. Colonel's orders. Lady wants the horse and the boy."

"I'll take the job," I said, trying to keep from shouting.

I didn't mind being second choice to Dandy.

The Seventh Cavalry became my home that next month with stables, stretching in long rows through the yards,

77

corrals that held dozens of officers' horses, racks of hay, troughs of grain, and tankfuls of water, fresh and clear. Dandy soon learned to stand still long enough for me to push the bit between his teeth and with the help of Burke one day, I hoisted the regulation saddle on Dandy's back and tightened the girth.

"Now, let's see you ride him."

It sounded more like a dare than an order. Right then I knew what Webb Cotter had done: He'd sold Dandy as saddle-broke to the cavalry! Some of the stable hands gathered as I led a prancing Dandy to the fence and looped the reins around a post. I turned to Burke. "I've got to get something. Be right back." I hightailed it down to the mess tent where the cooks were clearing away breakfast.

"Please, sir . . ." I'd learned fast to add "sir" to every word I spoke. "I need some molasses bad!"

The mess sergeant must have heard shivers in my voice because he handed me a tin cup half full of molasses and said, "Hope this does it for you."

I ran back to Dandy. There were more men, now, watching. I looped the reins around the pommel, dipped my fingers into the molasses and smeared it across his mouth. He started licking and before he stopped, I was in the saddle, reins in one fist and the other hanging on to his mane. He tensed, danced sideways almost into the circle of men, and stood quiet for a second.

"Please, Dandy," I breathed and we shot out of the yard, down across the encampment, me hanging tight, as the wind whistled through my ears. We swerved away from the last tent and took off at a full gallop .

"It's only me!" I shouted over the pounding of his hooves. "We've done this before. Don't you remember?" We were going so fast that he didn't take time to buck and all I could hope was he wouldn't step in a prairie dog hole and kill us both.

The wind swept through the buffalo grass, and up ahead I could see where it was cropped short, a sure sign of a buffalo herd. I think Dandy smelled them, because, after shaking his head as if to throw off his bridle, he settled into his uneven trot. I finally got him turned back toward the fort, but he still hadn't tuckered out enough to calm down to a walk. The tin cup had jiggled down and out the bottom of my shirt, and molasses was all down my front and across Dandy's neck. I was tired and sore from the pounding I was taking and thought about getting down and leading Dandy back, but if he got away from me on the prairie, Burke would have skinned me.

Nobody was around when we got back, so I took him to his stall and gave him a good cleanup. Either he'd liked our jaunt or he was hoping for another taste of something sweet because he kept bumping me with his nose every chance he got. When I finished, I went out and sat down by the door. I thought I was alone until I heard a voice.

"Never been under saddle, had he?" Burke squatted in the dirt beside me.

"Not till now," I answered, staring at the ground.

"Why didn't you say so?"

"I was afraid of how you might try to sack him."

He was quiet for a while, and then he said, "Don't see no need. He's saddle-broke now!"

At first I figured no one knew or cared about my wild ride on Dandy, but I found out that in the Seventh Cavalry, anything different from the boredom of camp life was news. The very next day a brand-new trooper, to judge by the looks of his uniform, came off the drill field and tossed me the reins to his horse. "Unsaddle him, Tad, will you?"

I wasn't a tad, and being called that by someone not much older than me didn't set too well.

"Ain't you the bronco buster?"

I shrugged and pretended I didn't know what he meant. I could tell he belonged to the Brindles. When Custer assigned companies according to horse color, the leftovers made up the worst company in the Seventh. They were the Brindles.

"Tell you what, boy," he said, stretching like he wasn't sure his back was all in one piece. "I don't know much about horses and I'm not much interested in learning."

"How come you joined the cavalry then?"

"Fella said I'd see the country, but all I've looked at is the neck of my horse and the tail of the one in front of me. What say you take care of old Misery for me?"

"That's his name?"

"That's what I call him. Government-Issue-Misery. That's his full name. He belongs to Joey Preston. That's me. I'll pay you if you do the cleanup. How about it?"

"What's it worth?" Burke had warned me that if I was going to tag along with the Seventh, I'd better learn to think "me first."

The trooper reached in his pocket and tossed me a coin. "Pay double that when we get back from the campaign."

"What campaign?"

"Down to the Territory. It's supposed to settle the Indian question once and for all."

I pulled off the saddle, which looked as if it hadn't been cleaned since it was new. "You mean the Indians are asking questions?"

"Must be." He took off his hat and slapped it against one knee like he'd been out on the trail for hours. "Anyway, the officers say we got to get rid of the Cheyennes when we find them."

I changed Misery's bridle for the halter from his kit. "Did you ever meet one?"

"Nope, not yet. How about you?"

"Yep," I said, putting the bridle away.

"Then how come you still got your scalp?"

"They're just people like us only they talk different."

He pulled at his earlobe. "All I know is that fellows say hunting them is more fun than running down buffalo."

It had never come to me that the cavalry was hunting buffalo and Indians like it was some kind of sport. "Maybe," I said, working on Misery, "they think Indians ought to look like us and act like us."

A bugle sounded "Retreat Roll Call." The trooper slid his hat back on, adjusted the brim, and reached for the lead rope attached to Misery's halter. "Ain't anything right. Ain't what they told me when I joined up."

I watched him walk away carrying the saddle and leading the horse. It looked like I had a steady income as long as we were in camp—making money off Misery.

One day Custer himself, dazzling in a blue dress uniform, gold buttons running up one side and down the other, came striding toward the stables. I was standing out by the corral watching Dandy when I heard him ask, "Are you Dandy's boy?"

I'd never been called that before, but I told him I was.

"Saddle him up, then. I want to try him."

My whistle brought Dandy trotting to the fence. It didn't take long to have him ready and as I handed over the reins, I said, "He's not much of a walker, sir."

"He'll learn to walk when he has to, if I know horses. He's got pride. I like a horse who knows how to hold his head." He swung into the saddle, touched his heels to Dandy's flanks, and they flew across the parade ground, Custer's Irish wolfhounds after them. A clump of hay loomed ahead and Dandy vaulted it without breaking stride. The dogs yelped, leaping around Dandy's legs.

"They'll spook him!" I heard myself shout. It was a chase. Hounds and horse and rider raced over toward the officers' quarters, then veered and sped across an open field, through the encampment and back toward the stables.

"Whoa, now! Steady, fellow!" Custer barked out in a voice that could have brought the whole cavalry to a halt. Dandy dropped into his dancing trot.

"I said hold it down!"

Even though the bit forced his head back, Dandy skittered sideways up to the stable door before he stopped.

The hounds still circled, jumping and nipping at his legs until one dog rolled on its back, legs in the air, and lay there. Dandy nosed him gently, rolling him on all four legs again. It was a game he and Splinter had played for hours.

"You picked a good one, Sergeant."

I turned to see Burke standing in the doorway.

"He's made for the hunt," Custer went on, "and he'd be a fine cavalry mount if I could talk my wife into letting me have him."

When the colonel left, Burke muttered, "The man's crazy if he thinks this is a cavalry horse. I'd rather ride a rain barrel than this critter. Here, take care of him." He nodded toward Dandy.

Right then, I was so far from Ma's "slow to wrath" and "understanding" that if I'd had a club, I'd have bashed Burke right across his stupid grin. Calling Dandy a rain barrel! I was even madder at Custer. Dandy was mine—on loan to Mrs. Custer.

I'd cooled down by the next morning. The autumn air was soft as a whisper when Burke routed me out of where I'd been soaking up the sun. "Round up Dandy and groom him good. Make that better than good. Custer and his lady are going for a ride."

"She's going to take Dandy?"

"Appears so."

"He's never had a sidesaddle on him or anyone in skirts."
I wondered if a horse could be court-martialed.

"She'll manage," Burke said grudgingly. "Now, get moving."

An hour later Dandy was tacked up, his coat shiny as a buckeye, and the funny little sidesaddle perched on his back when a trooper led Dandy's stable mate, Old Vic, from her stall and said, "This'll be worth watching. Wonder if the bay can keep up with the general and Old Vic."

"He'll keep up," Burke growled, "if the lady can keep on."

When we turned around, Custer was standing there dressed in buckskins with a campaign hat tilted over one eye, and his yellow curls falling almost to his shoulders. If a man could be pretty, I guess he was, except his eyes were blue and so cold they made me shiver even when he was smiling.

"You have him ready for a lady, Sergeant?" he asked.

"Yes, sir." Burke gave a careless half-salute. "Does she know he's got a hard trot?"

"We won't go far, just down around the stockade."

"Don't know how he'll act with the sidesaddle."

Custer nodded and said, "I know, but you don't argue with my Libbie when she makes up her mind."

"Make up my mind about what, Autie?" Mrs. Custer walked up to us carrying a thin black crop and smoothing down her bright blue riding skirt. With the sun shining on her auburn hair, she was a lot prettier than Custer.

"He's not an easy ride, ma'am," Burke said.

"That's because he's meant for dancing." She offered Dandy a lump of sugar and patted his neck. "Guess we're ready."

Quick as a cat, Custer turned, swept her up in his arms, and lifted her into the saddle.

Dandy was moving before she could find the stirrup, doing his little side step.

"Hang on, girl." Custer laughed "Hold him in."

She didn't scream or holler. Instead she talked to him, soft and easy, and kept tightening the reins until he stood more or less still. Athens told me once that in order to control a horse, you had to have as much sense as the horse did. Just then it seemed like Mrs. Custer was a right sensible woman, but Dandy must have realized he had something strange on his back. He reared up on his hind legs and when his front ones hit the ground he was off and away with Mrs. Custer somewhere up around his neck.

With one leap, they cleared two ricks of hay beside the corral and were racing across the parched parade ground, down past the line of tents, and out onto the plains. The colonel was laughing so hard he could hardly mount his own horse, but Burke, leaning up against the stable door, stood looking off in the opposite direction.

"Tell Libbie, when she gets back, I'll be up at headquarters. We'll brand him tomorrow, Burke, with the rest of the bays. We'll see how he weathers the winter campaign. I think we may have a match for Old Vic."

About a half hour later, Mrs. Custer rode up on Dandy. She smiled as Burke helped her down from the saddle, and said, a little out of breath, "I like a horse with spirit."

The next day Dandy was branded with the official US, but I pretended it meant "us" not United States. The government might own him, but he belonged to me . . . and Mrs. Custer.

The government took over, though. From then on, my job was to work with Dandy, adding weight to his saddle each time I exercised him—canteen, saddlebags, carbine sling and swivel, shelter tent, nose bag, picket pin, lariat—until he became as familiar with ninety or so pounds of kit and equipment as he was with me. I knew I was turning him into a cavalry mount, but I decided it might not be too bad a life. The troopers were always getting equipped and riding off looking for Indians, but they never ran into any, so they hunted buffalo instead. They even bet on who could bring back the most tongues. There was still talk about a winter campaign into Indian Territory, but I pretended it wouldn't happen and hoped, if it did, Mrs. Custer wouldn't let the colonel take Dandy along.

"Hey, you—Dandy's boy. General says saddle up that horse and bring him around. Mrs. Custer wants to ride him again."

"Yes, sir!" I answered. When Custer sent an order to the stable, everyone jumped. It was my job to get Dandy ready and deliver him.

It was a beautiful fall morning—the frost of the night before still glistened in the sun, promising one of those Indian summer days. I led Dandy, curried and brushed to a fare-thee-well, down past the troopers' tents and up to the colonel's quarters. One of his aides took the reins from me with, "Wait around back until the lady returns."

I walked around to the kitchen entrance and sat on the bottom step. Anyone who thought cavalry life was exciting never spent time at Fort Hays. The door opened behind me and I heard a swish as a dishpanful of water sailed over my head and splattered in the dust.

"Whoops! Didn't see nobody out here." The voice reminded me of Ma's, the kind that just by its sound made things right—like warm when I was shivering or cool when I was sweating. "That kitchen get hot as a fiery furnace on a day like this."

"Nice breeze out here, ma'am," I said, wiping the fine spray of dishwater from my cheek.

"I'm no ma'am. I'm Eliza."

"Pleased to meet you, Eliza," I said, standing up. Ma used to make me practice being polite so I'd know how to do it when I had to. So far, I hadn't had much need.

Eliza laughed a deep, throaty laugh and sat down. "You making me feel like a lady, but I'm just the cook so you might as well stay put." She patted the step beside her.

"I'm Caleb."

"Caleb? A spy sent into Canaan to look for the Promised Land."

She was right. I'd read it to Webb back in our Bible days. "How'd you know that?"

"I read. Learn by myself. So where's this Promised Land you looking for, Caleb?"

I knew she was joshing, but when I looked at her, she wasn't smiling.

"Cause if you find it," she went on, "let me know if they let colored folks in. I been looking for that place as long as I remember."

"Maybe it's in Colorado or out in California. If the railroad goes through, it'll be easy to get there," I said.

She wiped a dishcloth around the inside of the pan. "I been riding that hope train all my life, boy. If you find out that's where it's headed, buy Eliza a one-way ticket, will you?"

"Yes, ma'am," I answered. "Maybe if this talk about fighting with the Indians stops, things will get better."

She looked at me for a minute and said, "Fighting don't get folks anything but dead, the way I see it."

"I think that's the way I see it, too." It was funny. She didn't look too much older than me, but she sounded like she'd done a lot more thinking than I ever had.

She laughed again, stood up, and patted my head. "You keep believing that, Caleb. Now I got to get a move on. First thing you know, Mrs. Custer be back and wanting who knows what."

Seemed like Eliza and I just struck it off from the very start—maybe because nobody else listened or talked much to either one of us. As far as other folks were concerned, I was the boy who took care of Dandy, and Eliza was an ex-slave who did for the colonel and his wife.

One day when I was waiting around again, I saw Eliza out in back, sitting on the ground while she ironed one of Mrs. Custer's long skirts. Two heavy stones held down one side of the skirt while she worked on the rest.

"Here, Caleb, help hold this corner down. Never a minute that pesky wind don't blow. Tea sails off before I get it in the pot." She pushed the iron in angry shoves. "Sprinkle flour on dough, it disappear in puffs before I can put my hands to it."

I'd often seen her mixing her biscuits outside. "Why don't you do it in the kitchen?"

"Kitchen's worse than outdoors! No sink. No cupboards. Dust blow through the cracks. Now look at that." She held up the skirt. "That devil wind whip the ribbons to shreds. She cut off my head and put it on a platter for this."

Even if she wasn't serious, I shivered at the notion of Eliza's black eyes staring up from a dinner platter. One thing I'd learned with the Seventh Cavalry, people didn't always mean what they said or say what they meant, but it almost always sounded bigger than life.

"If you don't like it, how come you're a cook?"

"No choice. In the war I run away from the plantation." She folded Mrs. Custer's skirt and picked up the iron. "The colonel take me cause he getting married and need a cook. See, Eliza does what she has to do, to do what she wants to do."

"So what do you want to do?" I liked talking to her. She

listened to my questions and even answered some of them as if they were important.

"Save my money. I got a man back in Kansas City. He learning the law and when he finished we get married. Maybe I have my own cook."

She disappeared into the kitchen, and after a few minutes she came out with two sugar cookies for me and a kettle full of potatoes to peel while I lay back in the coarse grass and watched the clouds make pictures in the sky.

After awhile, she put down her knife and we stayed there, without talking. For some reason I couldn't understand, I began to wonder how Webb Cotter was getting along without me. I suppose it was because being with Eliza was kind of like being with Ma. I even told her that once. She said it was just the cookies, but she didn't mean it because when you're friends, you both know it's more than cookies.

In the evenings when twilight came, there was nothing to do but wait around until the bugler sounded "Taps" and everyone turned in. Once I wandered off behind the long line of stables, and there was Eliza, looking off across the dark land.

I walked up beside her and asked, "Is there something the matter?"

"No," she answered. "Sometimes I get just plain blue lonesome. Miss Libbie got the general. You got Dandy. I ain't got nobody. No picnics, no church singing. And I so tired of buffalo roast I grow horns and start to bellow before I get back to God's country."

"I know how you feel," I said. "Maybe it's because there's so much of Kansas. Everywhere you look, there's nothing but more Kansas."

"Everything come in such a rush. Lightning, floods, twisters. Listen at that wind down in the ravine. We just an island in a sea of buffalo grass. What wouldn't I give . . ." Her voice faded out into the night air.

The next day, though, when I delivered Dandy to the lady, Eliza was her usual self. She stood outside the kitchen door trying to shoo away a pack of the colonel's hounds.

"Chase those infernal dogs away, Caleb. A body can't cook with all their yapping and jumping around."

"Sure!" I shouted and pelted the dogs with clumps of dry dirt while she watched.

"Sit a spell, boy. Custers don't finish my biscuits this morning and you looking so skinny you'll blow away in this wind one of these days."

Eliza's biscuits, after the Seventh's usual hardtack, were a royal treat, and sitting on the doorstep, with the autumn sun blazing down, I felt like king of something. While I ate, Eliza ground coffee beans.

I tried to put into words what had been a worry on my mind for a while. "What does 'settle the Indian question' mean?" I'd heard the troopers talking, but I knew if I asked one of them I'd just get laughed at.

"Where you hear that?"

"Around the stable."

"I just know what the general tell Miss Libbie. He going

off this winter to find the Cheyennes somewhere down south."

"Why in winter?"

"Cause all the Indians, they don't do fighting in the winter. They hole up someplace and rest till spring, sort of like squirrels do."

"Then why doesn't the Seventh just leave them be?"

She stood, picked up the coffee grinder, started for the kitchen door, then turned. "It's killing time, Caleb. This place no Promised Land."

MOVING OUT

Chapter Seven

The very next day orders came down to the stable to reshoe all mounts and forge sets of new shoes to be carried along on the march. Later that same afternoon, supply wagons started rolling in with stacks of new tents, piles of heavy uniforms, rounds for carbines, Gatling guns, revolvers, spades, pickaxes, hatchets, currycombs, brushes, and new troops of cavalry.

"Where are we going?" I asked Burke as he paused for breath from barking out orders.

"We're moving south, first to Fort Dodge and then to the Indian Territory."

"Why can't we just let the Indians alone? They're not even around here anymore." There was plenty of land for all of us, as far as I could see, and as far as I could see, that's what I saw—more prairie than anybody could ever use.

"Progress." Burke spit on the ground. "That's another word for railroad." He picked up one of Dandy's newly shod hooves and shook his head. "He'll have these worn off in no time with all his prancing."

"How long will we be gone?"

"Custer calls it a winter campaign and it's almost November. You figure it out."

Months! It was hard to believe, but when they started loading the wagons with lumber, spades, shovels, grindstones, doors, windows, I knew it was true. This was going to be just one more longer, useless chase after Cheyennes who disappeared without leaving a trail.

It took a while to get everything organized and headed in the right direction, but when reveille sounded that November morning, the orders came to move out. Burke and I had our supply wagon loaded and ready to go and by stable call Old Vic and Dandy were tacked up. Dandy, of course, was raring to go.

"Never know which one Custer wants," complained Burke as he led the two mounts out of the stable and tied them to the wagon. "My guess is Dandy. Colonel will get bored and have to do some buffalo hunting on the way."

"I didn't know there were this many people in all of Kansas," I said, squinting through the morning mist at the columns forming on the parade grounds and spilling out past the officers' quarters and the guard house. "I'll bet there must be a hundred wagons."

"Four hundred and some," grunted Burke. "Eleven companies of the Seventh, five companies of infantry, and the

Kansas Volunteers, if they can catch up with us. Besides that, we're dragging along a herd of beef cattle and two generals."

"If I was a Cheyenne, I'd be scared," I said, thinking of Hawk.

A bugle sounded "Boots and Saddles." Custer, in buckskins, strode out of the mist, nodded toward Dandy and stood, drawing on his gloves and inspecting the wagon at one glance. I handed him Dandy's reins. He didn't even see me. Without a word he mounted and galloped off. Even though I knew Dandy was in front of us all, somehow I didn't feel proud.

We moved east on the Arkansas River to Mulberry Creek, going from river to river because those were the only landmarks. No trees grew for miles and there was nothing to guide us but hazy hills far off on the horizon. Sometimes we dipped into little valleys covered with buffalo grass, dry and yellow like a big rug, and climbed sharp little rises dotted with cactus.

"How far is it to where we're going?" I asked Burke. We'd been riding for miles without saying a word, except when he flicked his whip and shouted at the mules pulling the heavy supply wagon.

"Nobody knows."

"How will we figure out when we get there?"

"Somebody will tell us."

According to Burke's map, we made thirteen miles that first day.

Next morning we headed toward Bluff Creek, Custer

riding Old Vic because he said she was easier when it came to a slow cross-country pace. Then the landscape started looking sort of familiar and the farther we went, the more familiar it got so when I spotted a man on horseback coming to meet us, I crawled off the wagon seat in one big hurry. "Think I'll take a nap," I explained, hunkering down in the back of the wagon.

As the rider came closer, what I saw through a split in the canvas was just who I thought it was: Webb Cotter and the cow pony, looking as if they'd been on the trail all that fall. Splinter, his coat matted, tagged along behind.

The wagon ground to a stop. "Need something?" Burke shouted.

"Nope," came Webb's familiar grunt. "This the Seventh?"

"Part of it," Burke answered.

"That your horse?" He was looking at Dandy.

"Belongs to Custer."

"Belonged to me once. Sold him."

I held my breath. Dandy nickered and Splinter raced over to him, nipping at his hooves, circling the wagon and jumping up to touch his nose.

"Get back here, dog!" Webb yelled.

Splinter didn't pay him any mind, just rolled over on his back and waited for Dandy to nose him to his feet before racing off again.

Webb climbed down and walked over to Dandy. I quit peeking, squatted farther down, and pulled an army blanket over my head.

"You wouldn't have run into a skinny boy? Around thirteen, fourteen or so? A tow-head with brown eyes. Name of Caleb."

I stopped breathing completely and waited for Burke's answer, hoping he'd remember how I never forgot to care for Dandy, bring his water or portion out his feed.

"Can't say I have," he finally answered.

What was he saying? That he *hadn't* seen me or that he *couldn't say* he'd seen me?

Burke leaned back in his seat and gazed ahead. "Lots of lads follow the army looking for excitement, if you can call it that. Kin of yours?"

"Belonged to my wife till she died. That near tore the living out of me. Boy disappeared when I had to sell the horse." He slapped Dandy on the rump. "Been hoping he'd come back to me on his own."

Burke didn't say anything for quite a while. I swallowed and my legs twitched like I'd been running until he went on, "Never can tell about a boy that age. They get skittish. Like colts—you either gentle them or break them."

"Don't know much about boys. Can understand horses. Sons are harder."

"Maybe he'll turn up someday," Burke said.

"Maybe. Smart as a whip—he could read." Webb coughed, then said so soft I strained to hear, "Surprised how much I miss him."

I looked through the canvas again. Webb, without saying more, got back on the cow pony, whistled for Splinter, and moved slowly on the way we'd come from. Splinter hesitated for a minute and I wanted to crawl down and hug him. He'd have remembered me, too, I bet, but he finally tucked his tail between his legs and took off after Webb.

I stayed back in the wagon until Burke shouted, "We're fording a creek up ahead. Untie that horse and lead him across."

I was glad for an excuse to get out because it seemed like Burke was trying to hit every bump. "Can I ride him?"

"Go ahead."

He didn't even look as I jumped to the ground. I didn't look at him, since I was afraid I'd start blubbering if he asked me anything about Webb Cotter.

"Take him for a little run. He needs it. Just keep in sight of the wagons."

They were all lined up waiting their turn to ford, so, tightening my legs around Dandy, I took off across the creek. I looked back once, and Burke was watching me, and then I got to wondering. By the time we turned and headed back, I was dead sure Burke was testing me to see if I'd run after Webb. Burke was that way. He didn't put much faith in talking—just in doing.

We made twenty-one miles that second day and camped on the south side of Bluff Creek.

The third night we camped on Bear Creek.

"We'll cross the Cimarron tomorrow," Burke mumbled as he crawled into the back of the wagon. Soldiers had to set up tents, but we slept wherever we wanted. "Then we'll head along Beaver Creek."

"Have you been down here before?"

"Once," he grunted. I knew better than to talk more because he could fall asleep in two seconds even in a cactus bed.

We woke to a snowstorm blowing from the north in gusts so strong it practically ripped the clothes right off us. In spite of the blizzard, reveille sounded like always and before daybreak we were back on the march even if we couldn't see more than a few feet ahead of us.

"Why don't we wait till the storm's over?" I asked.

"Can't hear you," Burke shouted back as the mules, heads lowered, floundered through the deepening snow.

"How come we don't wait?" I repeated.

He turned and swiped the snow from his face with his big buffalo-skin mittens. "We got to get where we're going and set up camp in case of Indians."

"But we haven't seen any." I was pretty well giving up the idea of ever being a cavalryman. It didn't make sense to be in the middle of a blizzard looking for something that wasn't there.

"That's because they're smarter than we are. They're snug in their tepees like any sensible human should be."

We kept moving with only the howling of the wind, the squeak of leather, and the crunch of hooves in the snow. We rested at noon with a small ration of grain and some snow water melted over fires for the horses. The rest of us huddled around the heat, chewing cold jerky and washing it down from canteens tinkling with ice.

By late afternoon, the order, "Company! Halt!" finally rang through the whiteness. We had reached the banks of the Cimarron, ten miles from the morning camp. Custer rode up on Dandy, snow-covered, ice fringing his mane.

"He's a trailblazer if I ever saw one. Made it without a stumble. Rub him down and see he gets double ration. You'll have to be up with horses tonight. Keep them moving around so they won't freeze," he ordered Burke.

I took Dandy's reins and led him to the far side of the wagon where he'd be sheltered a little from the icy wind. He greeted me with his usual whinny. I measured out his rations, and as he ate, I rubbed him down and threw a horse blanket over him.

"Can he stay right here?" I asked Burke. "Instead of out on the picket line? I'll watch him."

Burke grunted. It didn't sound like a no, so that night as the wind continued to pile drifts of snow around us, I woke every time I heard Burke cracking his whip over the picket line to keep the horses moving. I got up twice and made Dandy move around, too. It was the only time I saw the dance go out of his hooves.

When reveille sounded the next morning, the wind had died and the gray dawn hinted at a clear day ahead. As I climbed down from the wagon, a trooper, wrapped in Dandy's blanket, crawled out from under the back wheels.

"Morning, Tad," he said, pulling the blanket tighter around his shoulders. It was Joey Preston. I hadn't seen him since we'd left Fort Hays.

"I think I stole something from Custer's horse." His scared look and the way his voice cracked made me think he wasn't even as old as me. "My tent blew down last night and I crawled under the wagon. Finally borrowed the blanket to keep from freezing. Didn't seem to bother the horse, but the general might feel different."

"I don't think he'll ever know," I said.

He unwrapped himself from the blanket and put it back on Dandy. "I'll do you a favor someday, Tad. Just don't tell Custer. He'd order twenty lashes and my head shaved." Then he started off through the snow.

I was surer than ever that cavalry life wasn't for me.

We moved out pretty good from then on considering the snow, and facing the sun, since we turned east when we hit the Canadian River. Right in the middle of the morning, though, the command to halt echoed back from the front.

"Now what?" grumbled Burke, climbing down from the wagon. I stayed put. I didn't even get down to check Old Vic. Custer was riding Dandy, so we were leading her, and Vic and I didn't take too kindly to each other.

Burke was gone what seemed a long time and I was beginning to have trouble with the mules that kept pawing at the snow trying to find a spear of grass. When he did get back, I knew better than to ask what was wrong. He'd get around to telling me sooner or later. We'd covered two or three miles before he started in as if he was telling himself about it. "Too many head honchos in this army! Standing there arguing over a trail!"

"What trail?" I couldn't keep from asking.

"Indian's riding south. Probably Cheyennes from Chief Black Kettle's village. Custer wanted to take out after them."

"Us too?" I didn't think the wagon could move fast enough to catch anything.

"The other general talked Custer down. They're going to wait until the Kansas regiment gets here."

I didn't want to hear any more. I almost wished Hawk had won the race that day and taken Dandy to someplace where he wouldn't be chasing anybody.

Two more days and we reached Camp Supply, only there was no camp—just a wooded bend in a river. As for the supply, that was the four hundred fifty wagons that made up our mile-long column.

"What happens next?" I asked. "Is Custer going to take out the Seventh?" I still couldn't get Hawk out of my thinking.

Burke gave me that look of his that said I was dumb as a fence post. "The Seventh is staying right here, protecting the infantry until they get a fort built."

"Protecting them from what?"

"Indians."

"But we haven't seen. . . ." I knew better than to go on.

The infantry cut six hundred logs—all in one day! And used them to build a stockade fence fifteen feet high—to protect against all those Indians no one had seen.

TO HORSE!

Chapter Eight

I thought maybe we'd hole up at Camp Supply for a good spell and wait around for some Indians to attack, but that didn't seem likely even to me. What Cheyenne or Arapahoe in his right mind would come at us with a stockade and guardhouse to protect us?

"So do we just wait until something happens?" I asked Burke after a day of sitting around and watching the infantry shore up the fortifications.

"The rest of the Kansas Volunteer Cavalry is supposed to catch up with us here."

"Where are they?"

"Lost, probably. Word is we're not waiting. Supposed to move out at a minute's notice and Custer's minutes don't last sixty seconds."

The minute's notice came when the bugle sounded before

dawn that November day, snow coming down so hard that there wasn't any room for air. Lines formed: scouts, supply wagons, pack mules, cavalry horses outfitted with full winter gear. The regimental band had all it could do to keep the brass instruments from freezing up.

Custer, bundled in a buffalo-skin coat, was everywhere inspecting wagons and checking supplies. Dandy, in full battle gear with Burke holding tight to the reins, tried to prance sideways in the knee-high snow.

Custer finally slogged through the drifts and grabbed the reins. "If this snow stays on the ground, I promise you we'll get our share of Indians." It was like he was talking about buffalo.

I shivered and it wasn't because of the cold blast that hit my face as I started for our wagon. Burke took time to salute as Custer swung into the saddle shouting, "Sound 'To Horse!' "

Someone else called, "Seventh Cavalry prepare to mount!"

Dandy tossed his head, hooves already moving.

"Where we going?" I yelled at Burke as I jumped up on the wagon seat.

"To clear out the Cheyennes."

"Column of two's!" The order rang down the ranks as a trumpet blared out "Advance." The band, riding their white horses, struck up "The Girl I Left Behind Me."

"Forward, ho!"

Custer waved his campaign hat and Dandy lunged to the

head of the ranks as if he, too, couldn't wait to clear out the Cheyennes.

"It don't make sense!" I shouted, but no one was around to hear, or maybe I just thought the words. And it wasn't just Dandy I was thinking of.

"Suppose we find more Cheyennes than there are of us?" I asked as Burke clambered up beside me.

"Custer's afraid we won't find any. He told one of his officers there weren't enough Indians in the country to whip the Seventh. Of course, he hasn't run into any yet and talk don't cost nothing."

The blizzard at dawn continued in blinding gusts that covered everything with ice as we snaked out across the plain in a long column of ghostly riders that appeared and disappeared in the swirling snow.

Burke had found me a pair of boots that almost fit, long underwear, two shirts, britches, a buckskin jacket that hit me where a full length coat was supposed to, and a pair of buffalo mittens. I crawled back in the wagon and snuggled down between boxes of ammunition, pulled some blankets over my head, and tried not to think of where we were heading.

At noon we stopped long enough to rest the horses, and then the columns moved on again into the whiteness.

We finally camped in a fringe of woods where there was enough fuel to keep fires burning. We even got hot food and coffee though the snow kept coming. Dandy, on the picket line for once, huddled among the other horses, rump to the wind, head drooping. Every other hour, Burke crawled out of his blankets and, like a sleepwalker, cracked his whip until the line of mounts became a restless, stomping herd.

Next day there was plenty of excitement. After three hours in the morning spent getting the supply train across Commission Creek that was a lot wider than its name sounded, we were resting the horses and mules when word came back that Major Eliot had found an Indian war trail that might lead straight to Chief Black Kettle's camp. I wanted to ask how he knew it was a war trail and not a peace trail but there wasn't time.

You never saw so many soldiers and wagon drivers and horses move so fast! It didn't take half an hour for Custer to have the cavalry organized, troopers supplied with ammunition, food, and a little forage for their horses. He ordered most all the wagons to stay behind, but he pulled out seven to haul ammunition and follow the regiment. One of them was us!

I hoped he'd keep on riding Old Vic, but no such luck. A sergeant brought her back and yelled, "Saddle up Dandy, and make it quick! This one stays with the supply wagons."

I had Dandy ready in no time even though my hands were shaking so bad I had trouble with the buckles. Up till now, what with no Cheyennes around except maybe in Custer's head, the whole trip seemed like a game. This was really happening.

Cradling Dandy's nose in one arm, I whispered in his

ear. "You'll come back, but I sure wish you didn't have to go." I wanted to tell him what to do when the fighting began, but I'd never seen a war.

Before I could finish telling him good-bye, the trooper came back, took the reins, and Dandy was gone. I wanted to bawl like a baby, but Burke had different ideas. He was already in the wagon cracking his whip and yelling at me and the mules. "Move it up! Move it out! Got a long, rocky ride ahead."

All of the Seventh Cavalry, except for one detachment that stayed behind to guard the supplies, streamed off across the snow-covered land. The band was playing, like always, flags fluttered, and up in front of everybody, with Custer on his back, Dandy led them all. If it had been a parade, I would have felt like cheering. It wasn't and I didn't.

Instead I hunched beside Burke and watched the Seventh start out. The snow was so deep, they didn't move near as fast as usual. I couldn't help worrying about whether I'd ever see Dandy again.

Burke must have guessed what I was thinking, maybe because I wasn't pestering him with questions. He shoved his hat back with one mittened hand and said, "Sooner or later we'll catch up with them. They move quicker, but they got to make the trail. Get some sleep," he nodded toward the back. "Won't be stopping till we get wherever we're going."

I thought I was so worried about Dandy that I couldn't drop off, but when I opened my eyes again, it was near sunset. I looked past Burke's shoulder at nothing but empty snow without anything to break it but the trail we were following.

The only noise was the crunch of hooves, the creak of the heavy wagons, and sometimes the howl of wolves in the distance. We stopped a few times to rest and feed the animals, but not long enough for a hot meal. I chewed hardtack and jerky, and washed it down with icy water from my canteen. I hoped Dandy was getting more to eat than me.

Once late that night, close to midnight as near as I could guess, we came on a camp where the Seventh had stopped. The fires had gone out, but some of the coals were still warm. "No more than a couple of hours ahead of us," Burke told me when we started out again. "Must have caught up with Eliot and they've all headed out together."

The snow stopped. The hills became higher, the creeks wider, even the stars were bigger. Through the rest of that long, long night, one hour blurred into the next. The Seventh Cavalry was somewhere ahead in the darkness and Dandy was leading us all deeper into Indian Territory.

Sometime before dawn the sky started to lighten enough to make out the shadow of hills on the horizon. "Where are we?" I asked, wondering if places like this even had names.

"Danged if I know," Burke answered. "If those are the Antelope Hills, we're close to the Washita."

I didn't know any more than before, but if the hills were called something, then we weren't completely lost.

It must have been another hour or so when we stopped again, this time to give the mules some rations and a chance to eat snow that was as close to a drink of water as they could get. The sun was up and we could see the trampled trail. With the wagons stopped and no whips snapping, the quiet stretched almost as far as the sky.

I was turning to ask Burke if he was ready for me to stow the mules' nose bags in the wagon, when from far away came a spatter of cracks and pops that sounded like fat hitting a hot stove. The sounds stopped for a minute and then came faster.

"Carbines! It's the Seventh!" Burke hauled me and the nose bags into the wagon with one jerk. Before I could open my mouth, all seven wagons were moving from a fast walk into a jouncing trot that made hanging on more important than talking.

A good thing the snow was packed down by the cavalry that had gone before us or we'd have overturned for sure. For all Burke's bad-mouthing Custer, he was in one heck of a hurry to catch up.

Ahead, a long low hill stretched up, cutting off the sounds of rifles. We slowed to let the mules, sides heaving, catch their breath for the uphill haul. I was glad the firing was muffled. With each gunshot I imagined Dandy trying to dodge bullets or arrows.

We were halfway to the top when Burke said a word he'd never used in front of me. I turned to look at him and saw an arrow stuck in the side of the wagon just above his knees.

His whip cracked louder than before and we lurched up the rest of the hill, the other wagons right behind.

On both sides, riding toward us along the crest of the ridge, Indians, faces painted, raced closer. "Hang on to the wagon if you want to hang on to your scalp," Burke shouted as we started down the slope on the other side. I clung as we careened, bouncing over rocks and cactus, rolling so fast that the tar-covered wheels struck sparks and started to smoke.

Burke's yelling almost drowned out the shooting as he cracked the whip shouting words I didn't even know existed. The ammunition boxes bounced back and forth while I wondered if they could explode all by themselves. I closed my eyes until we jarred to a stop, the mules lathered and blowing.

Before we could unload, troopers climbed on the wagon, threw ammunition boxes to the ground and grabbed shells, stuffing them in their pockets. I looked around and then wished I hadn't. Tepees stood in a circle, but the ground of what used to be a village was scattered with bodies, all of them Indians, mostly women and children as far as I could tell. Screams, shouts, and the piercing bark of pistols echoed between the hills.

The Seventh ringed the village, backs to us, firing whenever the warriors who had followed us came within range. It wasn't hard to see that there was no one left to fight inside the camp—they'd either been killed or had escaped or had been taken prisoner. Burke, almost out of breath from all his shouting, slid down beside me. "Looks like we're in the same fix they were a few hours ago. Now we're surrounded." He gestured at the empty lodges. "Wonder how Custer will wiggle out of this one."

A trooper bent over beside me and shoveled handfuls of bullets into his pockets.

"Haven't you killed enough Indians?" I asked before I could stop.

He looked up at me, face smudged and bloodied. "We finished off Black Kettle and his woman, but these ain't for more Cheyennes. They're for the ponies." He pointed to the far edge of the village. "Must be close to eight hundred."

"It doesn't make sense!"

"Custer's orders. 'Shoot them,' he said."

Then he was gone and another man galloped up, a second horse in tow. "You," he shouted at me. "The general says clean this horse up and get him some water. Not too much."

It was hard to know it was Dandy, covered with mud and dirty snow melting from neck to flanks. And his front legs, from hoof to shoulder . . . blood.

"What happened!" I meant to shout but it was almost a whisper. For the first time, Dandy didn't nicker when he heard my voice.

"General said he never flagged once." The trooper eased back in his saddle. "Says never was such another horse created."

I turned away, but the man was still talking.

"I saw it all. Custer led the charge and this horse cleared

the water in one jump. A Cheyenne had them in his sights, but the general finished him before the topknot could get a shot off. Then a boy with a jackknife came at him and Custer rode right over him."

"Did he get hurt?"

"Custer's fine. So's the horse." He handed me Dandy's reins. "Left the Indian flat as a snake."

"He killed the boy?"

"One less Cheyenne to worry about."

I knew right then that Ma's picture had it all wrong. There wasn't any peaceable kingdom where tigers didn't kill and where boys could hug lions.

I led Dandy toward the river, where I broke the ice and washed him, turning the water red as the soil that lined the banks of the Washita. Shots rang out. The killing of the Cheyenne ponies began. Dandy didn't flinch at the sounds.

The troopers saved enough ponies to serve as mounts for the prisoners huddling at the edge of camp. I hoped that Hawk's buckskin was there. Holding Dandy, I stared at the Cheyennes who had lived through the morning. They were all women and a few children who looked too mixed up and scared to run even if the soldiers hadn't been there. Behind them, troopers pulled down the lodges and dragged them into a big pile along with everything that had been inside—weapons, clothes, buffalo skins, food—anything that could be moved.

Custer strode up, grabbed Dandy's reins and shouted to one of his scouts. "Get that torched and hurry it up! We're moving out!"

I looked up at the hills surrounding us. On every side, out of range of guns, Indians watched us. A blast of heat hit me. The blaze of the fired lodges leaped high, turning the trampled ground to mud. Crackling flames almost drowned out the high-pitched cries of the women and the last dying screams of the ponies.

The battle of the Washita was over, but from the look of the hills around us, Custer was a long way from "cleaning out the Cheyennes."

With the band playing "Garry Owen" as loud as they could, banners flying in the wind, headed up by Custer, his scouts, and sharpshooters, the regiment moved out from the ruined village. On what was left of the ponies, the Cheyenne prisoners, under guard by two columns of troopers, followed behind our wagon.

Burke was busy getting us into our place in line, but I tried a question anyway. "Why aren't we heading back to Camp Supply?" We'd driven all one day, driven all night, spent the morning watching ponies get killed and tepees burned and now we were marching again—in the wrong direction!

Burke answered through clenched teeth. "Making sure them warriors don't follow us back to the supply train."

I didn't like what we were leaving behind in the Cheyenne camp, but I didn't much like what was ahead either. On the hills above the valley, warriors on horseback, hundreds of them, I guessed, milled around like they were trying to decide what to do.

"We're going to get shot at!" I yelled.

"Naw," he answered, urging the mules into a faster gait, "they might hit their women and children."

As I watched, a chief held his gun high in the air, and without shots fired, the whole band of warriors rushed ahead and away from us.

"What happened?" I asked.

"Going back to protect their own camps. Probably think Custer's got another slaughter in mind. This time them, instead of Black Kettle's village."

"Does he?" I wished I could stand up and let go a whistle that would bring Dandy galloping back to me—with or without Custer, I didn't care which.

"Wouldn't be surprised."

After the Indians disappeared, the regiment kept moving straight ahead. It was dark when we came on another village, but it was empty. Even the dogs were gone. There was no way the Cheyenne scouts who'd been following us could watch us any longer.

"Company, halt!" came the command, passed down through the ranks. "Counter march! Forward, ho!"

Burke struggled to turn the wagon around. "It doesn't make sense," I said. "What are we doing?"

"Custer's luck's holding. Made them think we're going to attack, now we retreat. It'll work this time, maybe. Not sure it will next time."

By what Burke said was ten o'clock that night we were back at Black Kettle's burned village. We kept up such a fast pace that I wondered how even Dandy could stand it.

After midnight Custer called a halt and we stopped for rest, building big fires from the dead wood on the banks of the upper Washita.

I helped Burke unhitch our mules, hobble them, and turn them loose. Behind us, like they'd been clubbed, the captives sat on their ponies. I tossed my buffalo-skin mittens on our wagon seat and followed the smell of coffee to the nearest bonfire.

"Here's Dandy's boy!" one of the troopers shouted. "Cozy up to the fire, boy, and have some hot coffee." He held up his own tin cup. "Here's to us! We cleaned out Black Kettle and his braves. They'll never fight, dress, sleep, eat, or ride again!" Someone handed me a steaming cup and as I took a sip I looked up at the trooper. From his belt dangled a scalp.

My mouth was full of coffee that my throat refused to swallow. The men started into the chorus of "Garry Owen," as I headed for the trees beyond our wagon. I spit out the coffee and threw up until my stomach quit heaving. I heard singing and laughing and joking like it was a big party— like all the killing didn't matter.

I poured the hot coffee out on the ground and watched it melt a black circle in the snow as light from the fire flickered through the trees. I was sick of the cavalry.

For the first time in my life, I understood Webb Cotter.

I was sick to death of the killing.

THE LAST DANCE

Chapter Nine

"Why make them come with us?" I asked Burke the next afternoon. "What's Custer going to do with them?"

Behind us and in front of the troop of cavalry that brought up the rear of the column, the Cheyennes rode on the only ponies that had been saved. Hawk's buckskin wasn't there. Around fifty women and children, some wrapped in bright blankets, slumped on their mounts like the life had been burned right out of them.

Burke settled back in the wagon seat, looked at me, and shook his head. "Caleb, you'll never make it in the cavalry. Keep wanting to know reasons for things. Nobody knows what the Little Big Man's going to do until he does it . . . and *he* may not know either."

"I could understand if they were warriors," I said, not giving up.

"He's got to have something to show General Sheridan when we get back to Camp Supply. There has to be something for the newspapers to write about. And one of the women back there is a sister to Black Kettle. Heard she's called Mawissa. She'll be good for ransom."

I wanted to know more, but from the look on Burke's face, he'd talked himself out, and besides, the signal came to stop and make camp for the night.

When Custer brought Dandy back to the wagon, for once he looked at me as if I might be human. "So you got through the battle, boy?" he said as he dismounted. "You'll be a trooper yet. Double rations for Dandy and I want to see him look his best in the morning."

Of course he didn't wait for an answer. I wasn't *that* human. He did stop, though, as he walked past the prisoners. He said something to an older woman wrapped in a dark red blanket and when she didn't answer, he tried using sign language. She didn't sign back, but the girl who stood beside her smiled at him. I figured that the woman was Mawissa because Custer never spent much time on what wasn't important to him.

As I unsaddled Dandy and measured out his rations, I couldn't forget the blood that had covered his legs just yesterday. If Hawk was dead, Dandy hadn't killed him. Custer had. And if all Hawk had for a weapon was my one-bladed jackknife, he hadn't been much of a threat. It didn't make sense why women and children got shot either. Wars were supposed to be what *men* did to each other.

It wasn't long before Custer, one of his scouts, and more than a dozen troopers were back at the Cheyenne campfire making the prisoners stand up and get in line.

Burke and I were sitting on the wagon tongue sharing hardtack and buffalo jerky so we had a pretty good view. He answered my question before I could ask it. Guess we'd been together long enough that lots of times he knew what I was thinking before I did.

"Just got around to searching them women for weapons." He snorted and shook his head. "Must have finally concluded that they might not feel all that kindly to the cavalry."

"You think they'd try to hurt somebody?" If they were as tired as I was, they wouldn't have the energy to do more than wish.

"When you've lost most everything, there's no telling what you'll do. Sometimes you give up, sometimes you fight, sometimes you get on with living." He yawned. "I'm turning in. No telling what tomorrow will bring."

Custer had moved on and the Cheyennes were settling down for the night when I wandered over toward them. An army blanket lay on the ground and a trooper was gathering it up to carry away. "Did you find weapons?" I asked, expecting him to tell me to mind my own business.

He must have been in a good mood, because he flipped the blanket open and laughed. "Have a look. Orders are to get rid of all this killing gear."

It was a very small pile. Those folks had been waked

before daylight and run out of their tepees straight into the Seventh Cavalry. I poked through the pile: a couple of pipes, some beaded ribbons, a bunch of hide scrapers, and one little doll dressed in antelope skin. I picked it up because it looked so sad and lonely lying there, and because it made me think of Topeka. There was nothing to cause harm to anybody.

"If you're looking for a souvenir," the trooper said, and laughed some more, "you don't want that doll. I've got a scalp I'll sell you cheap."

I put the doll back on the blanket. "No, thanks," I said, "I've got a scalp of my own." I didn't bother to tell him it was still fastened to my head.

When reveille woke me the next morning, the wind had changed to the south and in a couple of hours, the snow had melted clean away. It was like the blizzard we'd gone through never really happened.

"Should be getting there soon." Burke urged the mules toward a long slope ahead, but before we got there, Custer called a halt.

"What's he up to now?" Burke handed me the reins and crawled off the wagon. Ahead, the sharpshooters milled around and the troopers who'd been alongside us took off at a gallop for the head of the column. I didn't see the band anywhere.

When Burke came back, he didn't bother to take the reins.

"What's wrong?" I asked. Everybody was going some

place different, and even the prisoners who'd been following our wagon were herded past us and almost up to the crest of the rise ahead.

He didn't answer until he took out his bandanna and wiped his forehead. "The Boy General wants to make a grand entry to Camp Supply. We've stopped so the Osage scouts can put on war paint, and troopers can polish their buttons." He shook his head.

It took an hour but we finally got the order to move on. When they got to the top of the hill, the Osages began chanting war songs, shooting off their guns, and letting out war whoops that would curl your toes. The sharpshooters and the prisoners rode next. The rest of the cavalry galloped by our wagon, the sun flashing against their sabers, and all the time the band who'd gotten back together was blaring out "Garry Owen" again.

"You know," I said as we jounced along, "I don't ever want to hear that tune even once more."

Burke turned, looked at me, and grinned for the first time in the ten days we'd been gone from Camp Supply.

As we came over the hill and looked down the long slope toward the camp, I saw Dandy far away at the head of the columns strutting and prancing as if he was the reason for everything. Except for the prisoners ahead, it was like nothing had ever happened and this was just one more big parade.

By the time Burke had stopped our wagon, the Seventh had dismounted, set up their tents, and put their horses out to graze. I looked for Dandy, but he'd already been unsaddled and was so busy eating grass that he didn't bother to answer when I whistled to him.

"What happens now?" I asked Burke.

"In the army you either hurry or you wait." He sat cross-legged in front of our tent smoking his pipe. "We done the hurrying, now we do the waiting. General Sheridan will tell Custer. Custer will tell the officers and sooner or later, somebody will tell us."

I gave up on questions and wandered around the camp. We'd traveled so far and so long that it felt good to be able to walk instead of ride. Troopers sprawled in the warm sun reading, writing letters, playing cards, or telling stories about the Washita to anyone who'd listen.

On downriver from the main camp, the Cheyennes had their own setup with a couple of infantry soldiers standing guard. I watched Mawissa as she gathered fuel for her fire. She was younger than Cheyenne Jenny, and there was something about the way she walked that made her look taller than she really was.

After she got a whole bunch of dry limbs together, she reached into the folds of her skirt, pulled out a knife, and cut a limber green branch that she used to tie everything into a bundle. There was something about the knife, the way the blade was set off-kilter, and the silver-tipped ends of the case, that made my eyes bug.

I didn't stop to think longer. I ran toward her. Holding my right hand in front of my face, I moved it like I was cutting. "Knife," I said and pointed to my chest with my thumb. "My—knife."

She looked at me, shook her head, and walked away, her back straight, her head high.

I followed. I couldn't think of the sign for *friend*. Finally I remembered it and moved in front of her, linking my index fingers, only I had to do it over because I was supposed to start with my left hand and finish with my right.

She set down her bundle of wood. Her face was stern, but her eyes were calm.

I was fast getting to the end of my sign vocabulary, but I remembered one more that Webb Cotter had said was the first sign he'd learned. I put both hands in front of my shoulders, pointed my forefingers up, and brought them down in a circle so my wrists crossed. "Trade?" I asked, hoping she could at least hear the question in my voice even if she didn't know the word. Then I unbuttoned my shirt and pulled out the eagle feather Hawk had given me.

She didn't answer and her face closed like I'd melted into the ground, and then she walked away. I didn't know if she hadn't understood or if she was plain ignoring me, but I figured I'd have the rest of the winter at Camp Supply to find out.

The only problem was, that afternoon Custer reviewed the Seventh Cavalry.

On the parade grounds, the columns were at attention while Custer read in a loud voice from an official-looking paper. I heard a few words like "congratulations" and "your splendid success." Then a breeze ruffled the paper and I heard, "your campaign is just begun."

I turned to Burke who was standing beside me and the horses back at the picket line. "You mean we're going back to the Washita?"

"Seventh is. *We're* taking the prisoners up to Fort Hays."

"What about Dandy?" My words came out in a rush.

"He goes with Custer."

"Dandy's not a cavalry mount!" I shouted. "Webb Cotter said so. He was supposed to be Mrs. Custer's horse!"

It was the first time I'd said Webb Cotter's name out loud since the day before he rode off with Dandy.

Burke, down on one knee inspecting Old Vic's hoof, stood slowly, looked at me as if he'd never seen me before and, handing me a currycomb, said, "Get to work on the colonel's horse."

He nodded toward Dandy.

Right then, I started planning what to do when the time came. I knew it would have to be soon because we were waiting for a supply train from Fort Dodge, and when it came, Custer and the Seventh along with General Sheridan would move out.

I knew Dandy and me could pull it off. Back at Fort Hays, almost every week, soldiers got tired of army life and packed up and left. It was easiest for cavalrymen because they already had horses and saddles and field rations, so all they needed to do was mount up and ride off. Chances were they wouldn't be missed until morning roll call and by that time there was no use chasing after them.

I couldn't help but remember how easy Joey Preston pulled it off on our way down here to Camp Supply. He'd slept under our wagon that night and disappeared the next morning along with three other men. All Custer did was have a list of deserters read after roll call.

There was one big difference though. I was taking the colonel's horse.

While the Seventh waited for the supply train from Dodge and I waited to run away, I took to going to where Mawissa had her campfire. I brought hardtack and sometimes a little sugar or whatever else I could filch from mess. She wouldn't sign to me, though she always took the food. I hadn't given up on getting the knife, but it was no good trying to hurry her.

One evening, Custer got there before me. He brought Romeo, one of his scouts who could speak Cheyenne. I hung back, but they didn't pay me any attention, so I edged closer.

They made a picture almost as strange as the one Ma painted. The campfire burned bright and brought out the red of the blankets the two women wore. Custer, like always, had on fringed buckskins and that wide-brimmed hat, his blond hair curling out from under it, and his blue eyes flashing when the firelight caught them. Romeo was a Mexican with drooping mustache and a hat even bigger than Custer's.

At first I thought Custer was explaining that all the captives were going to be sent up north in a day or two when the wagons arrived, but then it came clear that wasn't what he meant at all.

"You both come south with me," he said as Romeo translated. "We find your people. If they come to the reservation there will be peace. You will help us."

I couldn't see what he needed the two women for. He already had scouts who could talk the language and do all the tracking.

They were talking to Mawissa, who wouldn't answer them any more than she would me. The girl who was often with her nodded, though, and didn't make any fuss, but maybe she was used to being bossed around or maybe she liked the way Custer smiled at her.

Mawissa stared at the fire and kept her mouth closed.

"Tell her," Custer's voice was louder, "if she wants her people to live, she will help us. Tell her to remember Black Kettle. Tell her the Cheyennes belong on the reservation."

It took more time and talk of killing before she signed back. She would go but only because she didn't want the girl to make the trip alone.

I waited till Custer left, but before I had a chance to catch them, the girl and Mawissa disappeared into their tent. I guessed that they had a lot to talk about.

I had better luck the next evening when Custer wasn't hanging around. Mawissa sat alone, her blanket pulled tight around her against the chill.

When I squatted down across from her, she didn't turn away like she did sometimes, so I knew, even if I wasn't exactly welcome, she might answer my signing.

"You—go—south—Custer?" I asked.

She raised both hands, palms up and shrugged.

"Find—Cheyenne?" I asked again.

She looked at me for a minute, turned, and spat on the ground. "Custer!" She spoke his name.

I thought to ask her if she'd run off with me and Dandy, but that was dumb. It was going to be hard enough by myself. She spoke to me in her language, but it wasn't any of the few words I knew. "Not—understand," I signed.

She shrugged again, like I was almost too stupid to bother with, and went back to signs. "Hawk—horses running."

At first I thought she was telling me that Hawk had escaped on horseback, so I signed, "Hawk—alive."

Shaking her head, she answered. "Hawk—finished."

I waited. That's the hard part about talking with hands. You can say only one word at a time and you pretty much have to stick to facts, not what you feel.

She repeated the sign for running horses and pointed to me. "You—Hawk—friend."

I figured it out! Webb said that Cheyennes were great storytellers, that after a hunt or a battle they spent whole evenings telling everybody in the village what had happened. She must have heard all about the race across the plains.

She slowly reached inside her blanket, brought out the

knife, and pointing to where the feather hung around my neck, signaled, "Trade."

We traded a knife for a feather.

She signed again. "Your—friend—my—son."

She showed no tears. Maybe she'd run plumb out of them. That's how it was with me after Ma died.

About noon the next day, wagons from Dodge rolled into camp with the supplies Custer had been waiting for and I knew that for Dandy and me it was now or never. Twice before I'd tried to get away, but with no luck.

The first time I had saddled up Old Vic because Custer wanted to get out of camp and go hunting for antelope. There was no need for fresh meat, so I guessed he was just in the mood for chasing and killing. When he was leaving he called back, "You, boy. Take Dandy out for some exercise, but mind you stay in sight of camp."

I would have left right then, but it was broad daylight, Custer had the saddle I was planning on taking, and if I didn't get back when Burke expected me, he'd have half the Seventh on my tail.

The other chance was after Custer had been out with the scouts looking for signs of Indians. It had taken all day, and they didn't find any, but it was probably more exciting than sitting around camp. Anyhow, he came riding up on Dandy, gave him to me to unsaddle, then walked back to the women.

Before I had time to talk myself out of it, I grabbed some

extra rations and stowed them in the saddlebags. Usually, I rode Dandy bareback, but I figured if anyone noticed, they'd just think I was doing something Custer ordered. I did stop long enough to shorten the stirrups. Custer wasn't very tall, but his legs reached a whole lot longer than mine, and I knew Dandy wouldn't take kindly to a gallop with empty stirrups flopping against his sides.

Right then Burke yelled at me to come help him for a minute, so I tied Dandy to a picket stake and went to give Burke a hand. By the time I started back, Custer came striding along looking like he'd been eating green apples. He untied Dandy, vaulted into the saddle, and jabbed his feet into the stirrups.

If I hadn't been so scared, I would have laughed out loud at the way he looked, his knees almost even with Dandy's back. I thought he'd skin me if he didn't bust a blood vessel first. He let out a string of words like the ones Burke had used when the Cheyennes were shooting at us and ended up with, "Get these stirrups down before I throw you in the guardhouse."

I moved so fast he didn't have time to ask why they'd been changed in the first place.

Now, though, with the supplies being unloaded and fresh troops joining the Seventh, time was running short for Dandy and me. I hunted all over for Burke, but didn't catch up with him till he came back to the tent for a smoke before Taps.

"When do we head back for Fort Hays?" I asked, knowing

it was a trip he'd be making without me. I felt downright mean about leaving him without saying good-bye, but I didn't know how else to manage it.

He didn't answer right away, making a complicated business out of refilling and lighting his pipe. Finally, though, he said, "Been meaning to tell you, Caleb. It'll be you going. Got it all fixed up so you can ride in the lead wagon."

"What about you? How come you're staying here?"

"I ain't." He looked kind of embarrassed. "I'll be following the Seventh. Guess I'm too old to break the habit."

"You swore you'd never march behind Custer again!" I knew he didn't like fighting Indians any better than I did.

"Somebody's got to look after Dandy," he said, making me feel even worse than before. "You stick close to Fort Hays, and I'll have him back there in the spring. Now get to bed. It's three o'clock reveille in the morning and we'll have to get the horses ready. He'll start out on Old Vic."

I meant to stay awake, but then I figured instead of worrying about making plans, I'd just *do* instead. Burke said that was how Custer's luck worked, so maybe it would be the same for me.

When the bugle blew in the morning, I felt like I'd just closed my eyes, and if it hadn't been for Dandy, I'd have sneaked a few more minutes in my warm bedroll. Outside the tent I couldn't decide whether it was darker than it was cold or the other way around.

Dandy trotted toward me when I whistled, but Old Vic snorted and tried a half-hearted kick till I got hold of her halter. I never did like that horse and wasn't a bit sorry that she'd be the one on the long march south.

Early as it was, the camp was in motion what with men getting their horses, wagons already trying to line up, cooks handing out last cups of coffee. Both Vic and Dandy knew something special was happening with all the noise and hurry. Burke came past to see if I needed help, but I had Vic ready for him to take to Custer's tent and was fixing to start with Dandy.

"Get a bridle on him and tie him to my wagon. Won't be leaving till midmorning. You'll be going around noon. I'll be back. Got a few things to say to you, so stick close." He started to lead Old Vic away and then stopped. "Before I forget, here's something to take with you." He flipped a coin to me.

I caught it and when I unclenched my fist and looked, I saw it was a half eagle. A five-dollar gold piece.

After Burke was gone, I reached under the wagon and hauled out the saddle I'd filched from a trooper the night before. I didn't dare take Custer's saddle. Anyway, he kept it in his tent. It was a bad trick on my part, but the trooper could get a replacement easy enough.

It didn't take more than a few minutes to get Dandy rigged up. He was as excited as me even if he didn't know what was going to happen. He plain liked to be doing something. I was almost up in the saddle when I thought better of it.

Instead of trying to sneak a ride out the back side of camp, I'd do what I'd done a hundred times before. I'd lead

Dandy straight down past the parade ground where the band was already starting to get their company together. If anyone was watching, they'd think I was taking Dandy to Custer. It was kind of like what he'd pulled off at the Washita—advancing when he really meant to retreat.

It worked because the only officer who paid any attention just said, "Hold him tight, Dandy's boy. Lose him and Custer will have your head shaved!" He laughed, but I knew he meant it.

The guards who usually kept watch from the stockade had been pulled back to help load wagons, so there was nothing to stop us. I kept on walking with Dandy dancing beside me wanting to go faster than I could manage. I followed the creek as it bent through cottonwood groves and hid us from the campfires behind.

When we'd got far enough so the sounds of voices and the cracking of wagon-drivers' whips had faded, I stopped and stood close to Dandy so I could soak up some of the warmth of his body. Ahead of us, to the north, the land rose gently beneath falling snow that glistened as the sky grew brighter. Maybe three days or so back to Dodge City and then we'd head west to Colorado. I'd told Eliza it might be the promised land. Dandy and me would find out.

I took a deep breath, grasped the reins, and was ready to put my foot in the stirrup when from back at camp came the sharp, crisp notes of a bugle.

Dandy sidestepped away, jerking the reins from my hand, his ears forward, his hooves dancing in the fresh snow.

"Here, boy," I called as soft and gentle as I could. Just

as he turned and started toward me, the bugle call "To Horse" echoed down the creek.

Slowly I moved toward him, eyes on the reins dangling out of my reach.

He stopped, head up, listening.

"Dandy." I tried to keep my voice from shaking. "Come, boy. Come to me."

It was like he was caught by two ropes, one pulling him back to the Seventh, one pulling him to me.

"Remember how I raised you, Dandy? The molasses? And I didn't try to break you ever, just gentle you. Remember how it was? How it used to be back before all the guns? All the killing?" My voice went on without me, just words with sounds I hoped would hold him.

The bugle shrilled again. "Advance!"

He froze, listened, flicked his tail, and wheeled. I pulled off my mitten, stuck thumb and forefinger in my mouth, and blew. The whistle cut through the cold wind like a Cheyenne arrow.

Dandy slid to a stop, front legs braced, sending up a shower of snow. I ran toward him while he stood, head up, his coat shining dark against the blue-gray sky. The band blared "Garry Owen," trumpets faltering in the cold, drums beating out the rhythm. I whistled again, even louder.

He looked at me for one long moment before whirling away toward camp, empty stirrups flapping.

Athens didn't know what she was talking about! She said if I never hurt him, he'd do anything I asked. She was wrong. I hadn't hurt Dandy, but now I'd never be able to gentle the killing out of him.

The music began to fade as the Seventh Cavalry started its march farther south into Indian Territory. Brushing the melting snow from my eyes, I knew there was nothing left for me here.

I'd catch a ride with the wagons going north. I had a half eagle in my pocket.

Maybe Webb Cotter still had the mare.

AFTERWORD

Some liberties have been taken with the sequence of events in this story, but much of what occurs is historical fact drawn from authentic accounts.

There really was a horse named Dandy, a favorite mount of Colonel and Mrs. Custer. He was purchased from a poor Kansas farmer. He survived the Battle of the Washita and other Indian campaigns. There was a Black Kettle, whose son was thought to be one of the first victims of the Custer attack on the Cheyenne village that winter day. There was an Eliza, an escaped slave who served the Custer household for many years.

Because Custer had ridden Dandy on the day before the fighting at the Little Bighorn, the colonel left him with the supply wagons and chose Old Vic as his mount.

Even so, Dandy was wounded during the battle, nursed back to health, and shipped across country to Custer's father in Monroe, Michigan. There, according to Mrs. Custer, Dandy spent the rest of his life dancing through Fourth of July parades until he died at the age of twenty-six.

DATE DUE			